MORE A Cottage Grove Novel

THAN A

FLING

Amber Nation

More Than A Fling

A Cottage Grove Novel

Copyright © 2015 Amber Nation

Cover Design By Najla Qambar Designs

Edited By Jen Akers

Other Titles by Amber Nation

<u>Brown County Series</u>

Not Alone

Runaway Love

How To Save A Life

Unconditionally

<u>Cottage Grove Series</u>

More Than A Memory

More Than A Fling

More Than A Friend (Coming Soon)

Prologue

2012- 2 Years Earlier

Dean

Maneuvering my car off the interstate towards my exit, I loosened the knot of my neck tie pulling it away from the confines of my throat. Summers in Dallas were excruciating and even though it was only eleven in the morning, it was already a sweltering 105 degrees. Once my neck could breathe again after being released from the silk noose, I proceeded to unbutton the top two buttons on my shirt before moving on to carefully rolling up my sleeves exposing my forearms.

It wasn't a common occurrence for me to be heading home that early during a workday, but as soon as I had received a text message from my wife, Kate, I asked my secretary Colleen to immediately clear the remainder of my schedule for the day.

Kate: We need to talk.

Four words was all it took for the flock of butterflies to tenaciously swarm around in my stomach. I strummed my fingers along on my steering wheel to the beat of the radio, trying to subdue my nerves.

Something about Kate had been *off* lately, and I couldn't for the life of me put my finger on it. Strong headaches occurring late in the evening, faint stomach cramps that had all but turned her off of cooking and cleaning. A fleeting instinct had me thinking that she was going to reveal that all of our hopes and prayers had finally been answered. After almost six years of marriage, I knew in my gut that she was finally going to reveal that she was pregnant.

She'd cried through countless hours of heart ache followed by seeing the best fertility specialists in the state of Texas, only to not be any closer to finding out any answers worth hearing.

That had to be what she needed to talk to me about, what else could it possibly be?

Slowing down my car and turning down our long, winding driveway towards our cottage home, the crunching of the gravel underneath the tires of my car did very little to dissipate my nerves. If anything it made the feeling more prominent the closer I approached. Bountiful cherry trees were in full bloom, leading me to my empty spot in front of the garage.

Only that day, it wasn't empty.

Not recognizing the vehicle as one of her few friends, my brows knitted together with vast confusion.

I came home early to surprise her, but it seemed as if I was the one caught off-guard.

Pulling up next to the Mercedes that was occupying *my* spot, I noticed it was a much newer and flashier model than my own. They definitely spared no expense when it came to all of the bells and whistles added-on. As a man, of course it would be the first thing I noticed and scrutinized. I wanted to wrinkle my nose at the over the top gaudiness of their oversized chrome wheels, but I also felt a pang of jealousy. Things had been a little rough lately, with Kate not working, trying to pay for my left over school loans, which the end was never in sight, and the copays for all of the specialists. A new Mercedes was wishful thinking but nowhere even close to being in our budget.

After killing the engine, I reached across the console and grabbed the handle to my leather briefcase, the same one I had received from Kate after I passed my BAR exam six years ago. I also grabbed ahold of the bundle of daisies I had picked up from the corner florist that was located next to my law office. I didn't want to come home empty handed when there could very well be cause for a celebration with her impending news.

As I entered my house I was immediately accosted by muffled grunts and moans floating from our upstairs master suite. I hesitantly placed my briefcase on the entry table located directly to my right before I softly closed the front door behind me.

Doubt was starting to crawl up my spine as I poised my foot over the bottom step just as I began to climb towards the muffled noises. I was beginning to think that the news wasn't going to be as hopeful as I initially thought. My feet felt like lead and grew heavier after each step I took ascending the stairs, and the sounds grew easier to hear the closer I got to my bedroom door.

Standing stiffly in the hallway just outside my closed door, I could feel my heart tumultuously thundering against my chest.

This wasn't happening to me.

But the increasingly loud, "Ah yes!" and "Oh God!" that was yelled in my wife's voice was proving that it was.

Sweat beaded on my brow despite the coolness of the house and my hand physically shook as I reached for the doorknob. I was waiting for the point when rip roaring anger would surge through me, but the only feeling that I could directly pinpoint was dread. Dread that I'd open the door and see with my own two eyes that Kate was cheating on me. We took a vow, entrusting ourselves to one another. Apparently I was the only one who saw that as sacred and wholeheartedly abided by it.

I inhaled a deep breath into my lungs, because I was sure once I opened that door what breath remained would be forcibly knocked from me. How did the age old saying go? There was no time like the present? Well, I was sure you wouldn't see it that way if you were about to catch your wife committing adultery in your own fucking bed.

I steeled myself and pushed the door open with such force that it smashed into the wall. *There was a glimmer of the anger I was searching for.* No amount of preparation could've readied me for the scene that was unfolding right before me. My wife, in all of her naked glory, was riding a man that I'd never seen before. The sound of the door jarring open must've startled her, so she had paused her position, wide, startled eyes now reflecting back at me.

"What the fuck is going on here?" I screamed, finally letting the anger overpower me.

"Dean!" Kate screeched while scrambling up off of the pompous asshole trying to find something to cover himself with. The bastard who just ruined my life quickly pulled the sheet on *my* bed over his lower half and actually had the nerve to smirk at me.

Here he was in *my* house, fucking *my* wife, and he smirked at *me*? This wasn't real life.

I now realized that the feeling in the pit of my stomach wasn't hope beginning to blossom, but rather apprehension not wanting to make its appearance known. Well, it was front and center on display now.

"Dean, let me explain," she pleaded with her hands held in front of her as she tried to come closer to me. I looked into the eyes of the woman I loved and saw that it wasn't the same woman looking back at me. "You weren't supposed to be here."

A menacing laugh ripped from my throat, "Oh that's rich, Kate. I just caught you fucking this moron and somehow you try and make it *my* fault? I thought I'd surprise you after receiving your text this morning, but apparently it was me who got the surprise." I threw the flowers to the side, not even capable of holding onto something that was supposed to be given to her. "So tell me, was this what you needed to talk to me about?" I asked as I flicked my hand towards the bed and the man who had yet to move from his position in it. Wouldn't you think the asshole would be smart enough to at least get some clothes on? I decided to let my displeasure loudly known, "Hey, jackass!" I yelled, my jaw tightening as I provided him with my attention, "You think you could at least put some fucking pants on or do you really have no respect at all?"

I turned my attention back to Kate as the guilt of her actions consumed her features as she feebly looked towards the floor. "Dean," she quavered, whispering my name and I hated it. I hated the way that it sounded coming from her lips. It was the voice of finality.

Her shoulders raised and her posture straightened as if she found a scrap of defiance, "I am leaving you."

Four words.

"I want a divorce."

Four more words.

The asshole sidled up beside her and tucked her under his arm as she continued, "I'm having his baby."

Those were the last four words that I'd let her say. Four fucking words that felt as if I had been dealt a major blow to my stomach and sent my world crumbling down around me. Words that were meant for me. It should've been, *we're having a baby*. Mind-numbing anger seeped all the way into my bones until I was seeing red before me. One minute I had my hand placed on the doorknob and the next I was connecting my fist to the jaw of the asshole.

A gasp left Kate's mouth as soon as my knuckles grazed his flesh and she was rushing to make sure *he* was all right.

Consoling *him* instead of *me*.

He quickly straightened his posture, removing his hand from his bloodied lip before letting his eyes connect with mine. He opened his mouth to speak, but quickly snapped it shut. He decided to go ahead and open his mouth again before saying, "At least you can represent yourself during your own divorce."

There you have it, ladies and gentlemen, my own occupation was being used to mock me.

I grew completely numb in that moment, my anger oddly dissipating. I turned on the balls of my feet and retreated down the stairs I had ascended mere moments ago. Who knew that with a series of four words and a span of a few short minutes my life would be changed and I would become a different man. My own occupation was thrown up in my face as if it were a running joke. I had picked that type of law to practice in order to help sad schmucks in what was suddenly my own situation and it ended up being an omen against me and my personal love life.

Hello irony, I'm Dean Parker.

Chapter 1

Present Day

Dean

"You need to come over as soon as you can," was all that was said to me before I heard complete silence on the other end of the line. I couldn't pinpoint whether Baylor sounded frantic or not and a call such as this in the middle of a workday was definitely out of the norm. Baylor Jenkins was my very best friend of almost twenty-five years and the thought of anything troubling him instantly had me on edge.

I hollered out to my receptionist and all-around right-hand woman, Beatrice, to reschedule my upcoming appointments and to hold my calls for the remainder of the afternoon. I grabbed my briefcase and all but flew out the door, thinking what a strange case of déjà vu this was.

The air was crisp on my face as I set out in almost a run towards my car, reminding me that I forgot my coat, but I was far past the point of turning back for it now. Fall was quickly approaching and it always seemed to cool off much quicker in Oregon than it did in Texas, where I had resided for several years up until this past summer.

A million different scenarios were playing out in my mind and they all tended to go in the negative direction. Something could have happened to Norah or Eden or even Petunia for that matter. That sweet yet annoying little dog had become a fixture in my life, even though she could barely tolerate me on her best days. As my hand gripped my steering wheel just a bit tighter, I remembered back to a few months ago when she absolutely hated me. Ever since we had to endure a thirty-eight hour car ride together and we got off on the wrong foot or –er paw, I'd made it a point to stay out of her way except to shower her with treats.

I knew how to spoil the females, ones with and without fur.

I pulled into the driveway to Baylor and Eden's house and put my Mercedes Benz into park. Although, I lived right next door, I didn't want to spend the extra added time in running over here.

The garage door was open and all of Baylor and Eden's vehicles were in the drive. I rushed through the garage into the laundry room, then continued on into the kitchen. That was where I found the both of them sitting at their kitchen table looking anything but frantic or in trouble.

They glanced up from a few notebooks they had spread out across the light oak wood table and at me with quizzical expressions and raised brows. I bent at the waist, placing my hands on my knees, trying to catch my breath that I seemed to have been holding during my entire drive there. I figured a moment of pause could be spared since everyone looked intact.

"What the hell, Dean?" Baylor exclaimed as I recovered my stance, unbuttoning the single button on my suit jacket and sitting down on an exposed barstool.

My erratically racing heart had almost been restored to its normal rate, so I slammed my open hand on the countertop to their island and just glared at Baylor. I threw the same three words he just said to me, back in his face, "What the hell, man? You called me in the middle of the day while I was at work telling me to come over ASAP!" I threw my hand in his direction, "You're home during a weekday but everything seems to be all right. What gives?"

Eden pushed back the chair she was occupying, stood up and came over to where I was sitting and crossed her arms in front of her chest. "Baylor, what did you say to him on the phone?" Eden looked to her fiancé and then back at me with nothing but underlying concern.

Baylor chuckled lightly under his breath before standing from his position as well and coming over to slap an open hand on my back. My mood had quickly turned sour at the fact that Baylor seemed to think this was pretty comical. My having to cancel the rest of my appointments for the day would put me behind schedule. He may not have been taking things seriously, but I did.

"I'm truly sorry, Dean. I guess I couldn't contain my excitement to ask you to be my best man."

Well, that perked me up. I propped my foot up on the spindle of the barstool and rested a hand on my leg, "You thought you even had to ask that?" I cleared my throat, "I mean, I was under the impression that it was already a given."

"I just wanted to make it official since Eden and I," he paused and grabbed a hold of Eden's hand, my gaze instantly honing in on their interwoven fingers. My heart panged with jealousy at the image of how insanely happy they were, "we've finally set a date."

"Oh yeah? That's fantastic!" I exclaimed, truly happy for my two best friends. "So, when will the big day be?" I was already pulling up my mental calendar so I could start fulfilling my duties as best man and planning the bachelor party.

What I wasn't prepared for was Eden to respond with, "Six weeks."

SIX WEEKS? My eyes bugged out of my head. It was the beginning of November, so that would ultimately put their big day about two weeks before Christmas. "Why in the world would you have it so soon?" I couldn't even fathom getting everything ready within a six week timespan. I had been married twice myself; my first was a whirlwind elopement but my other 'significant other,' who shall remain nameless, took months and months of planning every little intimate detail. Making sure the colors were right, along with the flowers and the cake, even the damn invitations had to be intricately precise. Which meant that it was all extremely expensive. This was Baylor's second wedding and Eden's first, and while she wasn't an all-out flashy woman I would have thought that she had a dream of how her wedding would pan out. Did they have ulterior motives for having this shindig so soon?

I eyed Baylor and then Eden carefully, while bracing a hand on the edge of the counter for either the answer that was going to shock the hell out of me or the blow that would sequentially follow my question... I narrowed my gaze and then lowered my voice to just above a whisper, as I leaned in closer towards Eden. "Are you pregnant?"

"Dean Parker!" Eden screeched as she drew back her right fist and landed it square on my collar bone. "No, I am NOT pregnant! What's the big deal that we are getting married in six weeks, it's what we both want, why can't you just be happy for us?"

"You're right, I'm sorry," I apologized as I gingerly rubbed my now throbbing shoulder, "congratulations, you two, I'm sure it'll be an amazing wedding for two amazing people." I had never had to backpedal so fast in my life. But all was ok when a smile spread across Eden's face, enhancing the glow that she had. There was a time, on two separate occasions, when I could've sworn that I had *the glow*. The underlying aura of being in love. But it was all just a strange fluke, a joke played on me by two conniving women who thought it was funny to see me suffer and my heart break.

"Who is going to be your maid of honor?" I already had a clue, just like I had assumed I'd be Baylor's best man. I knew this woman was going to be Eden's maid of honor, it was just the icing on top of the cake to hear her confirm it.

"Julia, of course."

Ah, Julia...

Julia Caldwell was Eden's best friend back in Nashville, where she had spent the prior fifteen years of her life before coming back to Cottage Grove for our High School reunion and reconnecting with Baylor. Jules was breathtakingly gorgeous, a spitfire, not to mention a complete and utter smart ass, and she grated on my nerves... She was definitely right up my alley.

A slow, sly smile began to spread across my lips, one much like the Grinch when he was up to absolutely no good. I then tipped my head back and released an almost maniacal cackle as I rubbed my hands together. This was going to be the greatest week of my life...or I mean, the greatest wedding of all time.

Chapter 2

Julia

I covered my mouth with my arm to stifle a yawn before I got back to rolling Mrs. Milstead's entire head in curlers. Since I was already lagging on sleep, I definitely should've rethought my festivities the night before I had to be in to work early. But just the image of Joe's, whose actual name escaped me at the time, perfectly sculpted chest, glistening with sweat as he was above me didn't allow my regret to surface for very long. A wide smile spread across my face as I recalled the most pleasant thing he did with his tongue, God that was glorious and for a brief moment I thought I was in heaven. Too bad I would never see him again. I smirked, shrugged a shoulder, then focused my attention back on my client.

Mrs. Milstead was a sweet old lady who came in precisely at the same time every week to get her hair washed and freshly curled. And my lack of engagement wouldn't even phase her as I always got to spend the entire hour it took to style her hair listening to her gab about her grandson and how special he was. And if he could only find the right woman. Perks of the job, I suppose. Sometimes I believed she was trying to set me up with him but in the back on my mind I had already dubbed him as gay. I wasn't looking for a man outside of the occasional hookup, such as I'd had the night before, nor did I need one.

Well, on the contrary, a little man action was often warranted, especially when you loved sex as much as I did, but he knew the stipulations beforehand. A one night stand never hurt anyone.

"Wannabe" by the Spice Girls started shrilling from my phone and a smile lit up my face at the thought of my favorite bitch calling me. I cradled my answered cellphone in between my shoulder and ear and continued to roll Mrs. Milstead's thinning locks. "Hey lady, what's up?" Normally my greetings to Eden were a little more explicit, but since I was at work, it was probably best that I toned it down a notch.

She didn't miss a beat before shouting out, "Be my maid of honor!" I quickly dropped the strand of hair I was working on and squealed with pure delight. Even though I was bitter and somewhat cynical at the thought of love, I was overjoyed that Eden had found hers through a second chance romance. She didn't even give me the proper amount of time to accept before she added, "Dean will be the Best Man."

"Oh," I grimaced while snarling my lip, just remembering back to my first encounter with Dean.

Eden had talked so highly about the duo: Baylor and Dean. Baylor and Dean, this. Baylor and Dean, that. And when I finally had the privilege of meeting them, while Baylor was every woman's fantasy, Dean gave a less than stellar first impression.

I was already having a shitty day because it was Eden's last day in Nashville before Baylor was whisking her away back to Oregon. Meeting Baylor was amazing; he was incredibly attentive to Eden, even noticing the little amount of hair that I snipped off at the ends. He only had eyes for her and it almost made me want to be jealous at the fact that she had found her happiness...almost.

The problem was when Dean began approaching us and he couldn't keep his eyes off of my chest long enough to even say hello. Don't get me wrong, I often like to flaunt my chest but since he was going to be taking my best friend away the least he could do was try to cover up his beyond obvious geeker peeking.

I quickly grabbed my cutting shears, clutching them tightly in my grasp and I didn't hesitate in voicing my displeasure to him, "Hey, chump!" I yelled, pointing two of my fingers towards my eyes; I could've expressed my distaste in the form of another finger signal, but I didn't think that'd be appropriate. "My eyes are up here," I said next, which instantly had him snapping his glare from my breasts to my eyes. When his eyes fused on mine I instantly regretted redirecting the focus off of my girls, for now I felt incredibly raw and naked. He stripped me bare with his titillating deep brown orbs. I tried to quickly cover my unexpected attraction to him, by becoming even more of a bitch. I perched my free hand on my hip and jutted it out to express that I meant business, "Didn't your mother ever teach you not to piss a lady off while she's wielding a weapon?" I added to the effect by bringing my hand that still had my scissors in its clutch forward, pointing them in his direction.

Dean finally cleared his throat after not muttering a single word since his arrival, crossed his arms in front of his broad chest and snickered, "You know, I do recall her mentioning something about that, but the only lady I see around here is Eden and it takes a lot for me to piss her off. Plus, her hands are free." He finished off his statement with a smirk, and I imagined that if he had one, he'd be dropping his microphone to the floor, thinking he had me.

I waited a beat, trying to think of some other retort to fling back at him, but as I glanced down at his broad, expansive chest, I lost all thought.

Well, damn...

I quickly recovered by assuming my defensive position, scissors still pointed in his direction, "You ass clown," I seethed. My chest was rapidly heaving up and down. "Why I oughta," I continued on before deciding to throw down my favorite pair of scissors on top of my work station and lunging towards Dean; I wanted to knock that cocky smirk right off of his face.

It took the strength of my best friend and her new fiancé to hold me back before I came to my senses and realized that I was better than that. So I straightened out my clothing and went about my business, trying like hell *to forget but failing miserably. That man invoked some serious feelings that hadn't been dredged up in years.*

It totally didn't help in the slightest that he was sinfully sexy. I honestly didn't want to have to endure his ass, but I supposed that since it was for Eden I could put up with him for a weekend.

"Eden, you know I would be absolutely thrilled to be your Maid of Honor." Mrs. Milstead long forgotten, I rested a hip up against my work station and grabbed my half-empty coffee cup in my hand. "So when is this shindig taking place?"

I tipped my cup up as she responded, "Second weekend in December. And we have so much planned that we'd love it if you'd come up the week beforehand, and maybe stay the week after."

There was blatant hesitation in her voice and I was almost certain that I'd heard her incorrectly. The sip of coffee I had just consumed, threatened to come spewing out of my mouth and would've certainly hit Mrs. Milstead's hair, but instead, I choked on it, forcing me to remove my phone from my ear until I could breathe regularly without coughing.

"What the flying Frisbee?" I said. She expected me to be around that…that poor excuse of a man for two whole weeks? I couldn't let my best friend down, but it was supremely hard for me to come to grips with this new information.

Then it hit me, they lived in Oregon and were getting married in December… Wouldn't it be frigging cold?

"Now don't you try and start lecturing me on getting married in just six weeks too. Dean actually had the audacity to ask if I was pregnant." She must've misconstrued the reason for my lack of response.

Rolling my eyes, "That's because Dean is a pig." The thought of them getting married so soon didn't even cross my mind. What a selfish cow I was being.

"You waited fifteen years, why should you justify your reasoning for wanting to get married so quickly? And besides, if you were pregnant and didn't tell me, there would be hell to pay," I said sweetly, and it was the God's honest truth.

"Woman, you would be second only to Baylor, and I'm only saying that because he is standing next to me." I heard a muffled exchange of words next which led me to believe that Baylor was voicing his opinion on her response.

"So why the outburst if you didn't mind about the close date?" She was fishing for something that I didn't want to disclose. I couldn't very well outright tell her it was because of Dean.

"Because it's smack dab in winter. I'm no freaking snow bunny, Eden." It was the best I could come up with, when in all actuality, it wasn't a downright lie.

"Jules, you aren't a stranger to the cold down in Nashville." She definitely had a point there, Nashville got its fair share of cruddy weather.

"Y'all don't get insane amounts of snow?" I questioned.

"This isn't Alaska," she balked. "Eastern Oregon gets quite a bit but here, we average about five inches of snow throughout the entire season."

My mind began to wander back to her asking for me to stay a week after the wedding as well. "Are y'all not going on a honeymoon right after the wedding? You asked me to stay a week afterwards as well, I guess I'm confused."

"Well, with the holidays approaching, Baylor can't take any extra time off besides the two days prior to the wedding until after January, so we will just go then."

After confirming a few more details I had to quickly let her go so I could finish up on Mrs. Milstead's hair; poor woman had fallen asleep in her chair. Eden had definitely calmed my nerves about being away from home during the winter season. That would be all I needed, to be stranded in one place with Dean right next door...

Chapter 3

Five Weeks Later

Dean

Pulling down the hood on my raincoat, I walked out of the confines of my nice warm and dry living room, into a torrential downpour. Leave it to Oregon to be the beginning of winter and it be pouring down rain. Before I stepped off of my front porch, I looked down at my phone once again to read Baylor's 911 text.

Baylor: Come over ASAP! We've got an emergency.

I'd learned since that day five weeks ago not to take Baylor's "emergencies" at face value. At this point so close to the wedding, Eden may have chipped a nail, or maybe her favorite Aunt Edna wouldn't be able to attend and she was freaking out. So, I decided to take my time and walk down my driveway and along the sidewalk so I didn't get my boots muddy tracking through the mucky lawn.

Going in through the soon to be Mr. and Mrs. Jenkins' garage as I always did, I ran into Baylor as soon as I entered the laundry room that led to the kitchen.

Removing my hood for the time being, I asked a frantic looking Baylor, "What's the *emergency* this time?"

"Eden is freaking out about the centerpieces, they aren't turning out how she wants them."

Do you recall my earlier statement saying that Eden was normally pretty chill and mellow when it came to things and I didn't think she would go all psycho bride? Yeah, she wasn't one hundred percent there, but it wasn't looking too promising that she wouldn't be there soon.

"What the hell are you calling me for? I'm not decoration savvy. Tell her to call her mom." I still wasn't completely sure why she wanted to make several of the decorations herself, it wasn't like they really needed to skimp and save money. Eden's mom, Bette, had evidently been saving up for her only child's wedding since the day she was born, and since Eden was now almost thirty-four, she had a pretty hefty wedding fund.

Lately I'd made it a point to stay at home because Eden had been a stressed and emotional mess. She was liable to crack at any moment and I didn't want to end up in the crossfire. So, I was hoping that I'd be safe and sound one hundred feet away in the confines of my own house.

"She has called Bette and she's on her way. But with Eden stressed and freaking out I can't leave her. So that's where you come in." I was confused, what exactly was he asking me to do? His eyes darted around the kitchen, looking everywhere but at me. I could detect his hesitation. "I need you to go pick up Julia from the airport."

I busted out laughing, because if he was looking for a way to get me he totally succeeded. "Yeah, right," I said not believing that he actually wanted me to pick up the woman who had threatened me with a pair of haircutting scissors. Granted, she wasn't completely in the wrong, but you get the gist.

The only problem was, he wasn't laughing along with me at his little joke. "I'm totally serious," he muttered with pleading eyes. Although I wasn't quite ready to see Miss Sassypants herself yet, I couldn't tack on any extra added stress to Baylor and Eden, so I reluctantly agreed.

I dashed into the airport, barely escaping the torrential downpour, and went straight for the airline itinerary board to make sure Julia's plane was still on time. I was willing to start completely over and let the past stay in the past, as long as she was. Which was why I was a gentleman enough to come into the airport and offer to help her out with her luggage.

I hung out near the baggage claim, where soon enough Julia would make her appearance.

I didn't have to wait long before I caught a glimpse of her waiting by the baggage carousel and heaving her big-ass luggage to the floor. Once she stood upright again and glanced my way she literally took my breath away. Something about her made me want her with every fiber of my being. Even after being on a plane for several hours she looked as if she had walked right off a page of a magazine; that was until she came closer towards me and opened her mouth.

"Why in the hell are you here?" She sneered in my direction, with venom and annoyance.

So much for turning over a new leaf and being gentlemanly.

I shoved my hands in my pockets and rolled back on my heels, "Do you think I actually volunteered for this?"

She took just a brief second to peruse my body, so quick that she probably didn't think I noticed. But I noticed, oh yeah I did.

"Knowing you," she turned up a side of her freshly painted lips, "more than likely," she said flatly.

"Yeah, because chauffeuring your ass around was high on my bucket list." I made a motion to check off that next item on my imaginary list.

"Oh please," she huffed. "This is probably the most excitement you've seen in a month."

"No, that award definitely goes to Eden. She's teetering on the verge of a breakdown."

Her eyes softened at the mention of her friend and all the stress she was enduring. Perhaps there was a heart placed in the cold cavity in her chest. "Well, then what are we standing around here gabbing for then? I have a best friend to help!" She pivoted on her heel and began walking towards the exit doors of the airport, giving me an unabashed view of her fine ass as she sashayed away from me.

Right before she reached the exit doors, I came up and stopped in front of her, ready to burst her bubble. Looking down at her immaculate outfit, including what I would guess to be four-inch heels, I said, "I see you made sure to bring your winter coat, but I hope you packed rain boots. It'll suck trying to walk to my car in the pouring rain in those heels," I pointed down to her stunning footwear that I just couldn't help picturing wrapped around my waist. Even though she drove me crazy with her smart ass remarks, I was a man after all and I wasn't ashamed to admit that I found her extremely attractive.

Her eyes went wide and I had to try my hardest to hold back my laughter that was undoubtedly threatening to erupt. "No...I didn't even think about it. Are you parked far?"

"At the end of the loading/unloading zone." Her face immediately fell following my words, this was just too much fun.

"Well, can you pull my luggage?" That was what I had initially come in for, but since she wanted to start off by being a bitch, those weren't my intentions any longer.

"Ah, sorry," I replied, acting a bit sympathetic. "An independent woman such as yourself doesn't need any help from a *man*."

"Ugh," she stomped one of her heels against the concrete floor, making the sound echo throughout the lobby. "I really hate you," she bit out between her clenched teeth.

21

"Oh, the feeling is definitely mutual," I smiled smugly to myself, pulled up the hood to my coat, readjusted, and patted the umbrella that was resting in the inside pocket of my jacket. I chuckled under my breath. If she knew that I had an umbrella in my possession, she would no doubt change her tune. But where would be the fun in that? I'd just keep that nugget of information to myself.

Chapter 4

Julia

Watching Dean's windshield wipers' reluctant assault against the clamoring rain drops as they hit his car, I couldn't help but continue to stew over our earlier altercation. I didn't know why this man grated on my nerves so badly, or what was worse, why I let him. He was just a cocky prick who I shouldn't even be paying attention to, but there was just something about him that I couldn't exactly pinpoint. There was no denying my attraction to the man but I absolutely loathed him. I didn't know whether I wanted to flatten his face with a chair or kiss the ever-loving shit out of him. It usually took a lot for a man to rile me up but all Dean had to do was give me a single, solitary look and I was raring to go with my claws out.

So, I was sitting there, sticking to his leather seats due to my drenched clothing, with rain-soaked strands of hair flat against my face. I was almost positive that I looked like a drowned rat.

Dean threw me off guard by picking me up, and I wasn't one to be a fan of surprises. But when he explained to me why he was summoned to come pick me up, I was ready to get to Eden as fast as I could.

"Can't this piece of junk go any faster?" I knew that I should just shut my mouth but I was anxious to take some of the load off of Eden's shoulders, and give Baylor a well-deserved break.

"Piece of junk? Listen, I know my car isn't brand new or even close to your high standards, but it is getting you from point A to point B, so I suggest you just sit back and relax sweetheart, because I know how to drive on these roads in the rain, and it's completely obvious that you don't." He didn't miss a beat, continuing to berate me, "If you would like to make it to Eden's house in one piece without hydroplaning or getting into an accident it may be best that you shut your trap." His hands were tightening their grip on the steering wheel and I instantly knew that I had gone too far. My own nerves were just getting the better of me and I was taking it out on him and his car.

Forcing myself to relax, I looked around at the different features inside the small space, it really was nice. Not over the top for some flashy lawyer, but just enough for a guy to make a statement that he had a steady and dependable law practice. I mentally chided myself for angering him further in the midst of taking me to my friend, and I found myself wanting to cover his hand with mine and apologize. I quickly nixed the idea, but it still didn't stop me from thinking about it.

The rest of the drive remained uneventful, simply put, meaning not a single word was exchanged between the two of us. It took us a little longer to arrive with the rain, but soon enough Dean was pulling into what I assumed was Baylor and Eden's driveway.

After putting his car in park, he wasted no time at all before getting out of the driver's seat and heading towards the trunk. I wanted to somehow redeem myself and show that I wasn't always such a diva so I quickly followed suit and met him at the back of his car. The rain had finally let up, but by that time so much damage had already been done to my outfit and hair that I didn't even care. He pulled out my large rolling suitcase and sat it on the ground, "Thank you," I said in a soft voice and went to grab for the handle when our eyes briefly met and a look of gratitude was exchanged.

My hand accidently brushed his and a rush hit me straight to my core. My touch lingered on his and he was the first to pull away as he said, "This way," he motioned with his head as he made his way in through Eden's garage. I found myself following him once again as we entered into a laundry room, I rested my suitcase right nside the entrance and quickly rid myself of my wet coat and slipped out of my shoes.

Running my fingers through mv now curly wet strands, I decided that this was going to be as good as it got and went into the kitchen to try and find my stressed best friend.

Sitting at the kitchen table which I knew to be *the table* was Eden; she had her fingers shoved into her hair and worry lines marring her face. Baylor had a hand perched on her back and was leaning over her, trying to soothe her frayed nerves. I could tell by his rigid stance and soothing tone that Eden was indeed teetering on the edge of a breakdown. Eden's mom Bette was seated on the other side of the table with a scared expression on her face as if she had been scolded by her only child.

Bette was the first to notice me approach, so I decided that it was time to let my presence be known. "I'ⲅ here! Let all the worrying subside!" I said and opened my arms wide as soon as Eden looked up from the table. The moment her eyes met mine all sigrs of worrying immediately dissipated.

She scooted back her chair from the table, causing Baylor to jump out of the way, and ran to give me a hug with the biggest smile gracing her face. She clung to me tightly and it was in that moment, hugging my best friend, that I realized just how much missed seeing her every day. For the past several years she had been my constant rock, helping me get over Paul, my second failed marriage. It wasn't an easy process, but with Eden by my side it made things a bit more bearable.

"Are you hanging in there, sweet pea?" I whispered in her ear as I gave a comforting rub up and down her back.

"Oh Jules, I'm so glad to see you. The centerpieces are falling apart, I'm losing my mind." She pulled back away from me just far enough for me to cup her face in my hands; without the height of my heels I was several inches shorter than Eden, which meant Dean was practically a giant as he stood next to me. She roved her eyes over my saturated clothing. "Why on earth are you soaking wet?"

I glanced to the right at Dean who had another smug look on his face and rolled my eyes in his direction. "Don't you worry about me, although some may perceive me as the Wicked Witch of the West, it's proven now that I don't melt." I bounced the tip of my finger off the end of her nose before I pulled out of her embrace. "Now, planning a wedding is stressful enough, why on earth are you putting together your own centerpieces?"

"I wanted to do them myself, I found so many different beautiful pieces on Pinterest and thought that they'd be easy enough to accomplish myself." This sounded like Eden's hair color catastrophe all over again. The reason Eden and I met in the first place was because she thought she could attempt to color her own hair and ended up sprinting to my chair so I could reverse the hideous orange color that was the final result.

"Eden, Eden, Eden…" I ran my hand along the top of her shoulder, in a calming way. "Preparing for your wedding is stressful enough, you don't need to add anything on top of that. I know you aren't used to delegating tasks out to people," Placing my hand on my chest, I continued, "so it's lucky for you that I am." I looked past Eden's shoulder and saw Baylor visibly relax at the mere mention of me taking charge. "Now, let me see your list of everything that is done and what still needs to be handled."

Eden's eyes went wide before scurrying back to the kitchen table to retrieve her notebook. She approached me slowly as if she was afraid of what exactly I'd see on the pages. It wasn't any secret that I had two marriages under my belt, and the fact that they were both failed was a moot point. The truth was that I knew what I was doing and there was no doubt in my mind that I could handle whatever curveball she threw at me.

Taking the list in my hands and flipping through her jotted notes, I wasn't expecting to see a lot of garbled nonsense and that hardly anything was accomplished. No wonder the girl was on the verge of needing a straightjacket.

"Seriously, Eden?" I sighed, closing my eyes and trying to calm my nerves before a headache set in.

Breathe, Julia, you can do this.

And immediately I snapped into action. "Momma Bette, do you think you can handle the centerpieces or do I need to make some calls?" I asked sternly, as my no-nonsense attitude slid firmly into place.

"I'll call Baylor's mom, Stella, and have her come over right away to help me. If I have to I'll reach out to my book club, but all of the décor will be finished today." That was exactly what I wanted to hear and she wasted no time before moving into the other room to call Stella to get her in on the action.

"Baylor and Dean, you two head on over to the place that is taking care of the catering. I want a finalized menu with a signed contract back to me by this evening." Dean pushed himself off of the counter on which his hip rested and saluted me. I narrowed my eyes at him, biting my tongue. That chair-in-the-face scenario was looking more and more promising.

"Eden and I will head on over to the bakery and get this cake finalized. I'm assuming the church and reception hall are booked and ready to go?" I was afraid to even look in Eden's direction. If that huge portion wasn't done, I was going to pull my own hair out, but Eden quickly assured me that everything was good to go there. "Ok, I need to get out of these wet clothes, Eden," I turned to her, "I hope you have an extra pair of rain boots or we will be stopping by someplace to get some." It was utterly a shame that I couldn't go out shopping in my heels but within the great state of Oregon I guess I'd have to make my fashion statement without shoes.

A young girl's voice spoke from behind, startling me and my thinking, "What do you want me to do?" I turned around completely forgetting about Norah, Baylor's twelve-year-old daughter.

"Uh," I was completely at a loss. "You can go with your dad and make sure that they get the menu right." I didn't know what else for the little bugger to do, and I absolutely didn't want her in my hair.

Her face fell, "I wanted to go with you and Eden to pick out the cake."

I didn't want the poor girl to cry, but there was something about me that I supposed that I should make abundantly clear.

I didn't do kids.

EVER.

I groaned on the inside and tried to contort my face to form something that resembled a smile. "Ok, Eden," I brought one hand to my hip, then motioned my other towards Norah, "do you need to pack a diaper bag for the child?"

Dean barked out a scoff. "Julia, she's twelve years old for Christ's sake, she doesn't need to be spoon fed and I'm sure she was potty trained at least ten years ago." He hooked an arm around Norah's neck and rustled up her poker straight hair, "Come on, Norah Bean, you can ride up front in the Benz and we'll shove your dad in the backseat."

Baylor, Dean, and Norah vacated the kitchen and I glanced at Eden who had her eyes narrowed at me.

"What?" I feigned ignorance. Eden knew my stance on children, but I guess I needed to get over my fear of tiny humans at least for the time I was there. "Oh I'm sorry, I'll try harder. Now could you please point me to my room so I can get out of these clothes?"

Chapter 5

Julia

Two hours later and we were pulling back into Baylor and Eden's driveway. Things at Sandy's Bakery went better than I could have imagined. Eden picked out the flavor of cake and the design in record time and I was just happy that we were able to mark something off of her list of things to be accomplished.

"Julia, I'm so glad that you're here." She snapped her fingers as if she just remembered something important. "In the midst of everything going on, I forgot to mention to you that Baylor and I will be leaving right after the wedding for our honeymoon." I opened my mouth to object but Eden steamrolled right over me, "Now, I know that wasn't the original plan, but Baylor's boss surprised us with it and insisted that he take the time off to go. We just couldn't say no. Norah will be splitting her time between my parents and Stella that week, so you really could just stay in the house until it was time for you to go back to Nashville. I'm sure Dean would be more than happy to take you back to the airport."

That was my moment to interject. "Stop right there," I threw up a hand. "Dean will NOT be taking me anywhere, I am more than fine with taking a cab. And don't you worry about me, this is your honeymoon. I may stay because some downtime is more than needed, but I also may just see if I can change my flight." Shrugging my shoulder, to show I wasn't affected in the least, I continued on. "No biggie at all, you just need to be able to relax and enjoy your honeymoon."

The answer seemed to tide her over but it wouldn't be Eden's nature if she didn't worry about me. And I knew just in her demeanor and the long sigh she released that she wished that Dean and I would get along. I was going to try my best to avoid the man so that the rest of the week could go smoothly for her without me murdering anyone.

We headed back into the house and saw that the guys along with Norah were gathered around the kitchen table. Bette and another woman who I assumed was Stella were busy in the living room with fake flowers strewn all over the place.

"Ok, everything on our end is finished," Baylor said, sliding the contract across the table towards me. I picked up the paper and placed it along with my little folder of important items. During this process Dean's head was trained down not even acknowledging my presence at all and Norah was giving me sideways glances.

"Perfect." I clasped my hands together in front of me, "Now how about we relieve some stress and go out tonight?" I looked at Eden, meaning to only be asking her, "I've wanted to go to Tillie's Tavern since you've told me about it."

Dean finally perked up from his deeply interested stare at the table and looked directly at me with a sly smirk, then promptly turned to Baylor, pretending to scratch his chin, "That actually doesn't sound like a bad idea, I think we all can take a little break."

The tension in the room instantly increased, even to the point that Norah felt the pressure. So she quickly scooted out from the table, "I think I'm going to help Mimi and Granny in the living room," she said quickly as she scurried away.

Dean thought he was going to rile me up, but he would soon realize that it took more than a self-invitation to do so. I crossed my arms in front of my chest, "Fine by me," I forced a smile, "the more the merrier." I narrowed my eyes his way before turning and leaving the kitchen and heading for my bedroom. If he was going to be in attendance this evening, I had to put together a killer outfit to make him eat his words.

Since it was still raining outside I decided to forgo the usual dress I would've worn for the evening and settled on jeans with heeled boots.

I'm normally not a big jeans person, basically living in either dresses or leggings. But if I did say so myself, being paired with my gray stiletto boots and an off-the-shoulder gray shirt, my outfit was fabulous.

My heels gave me some semblance of height, which would only boost my confidence level. My small stature really dragged down my big personality.

I was thrilled when we finally arrived at Tillie's, because being forced to endure the entire car ride in the backseat was brutal.

Oh, did I mention that I had to share it with Dean?

The man was a giant anyway, compared to my five-foot-two stature, but being forced to cram himself in a limited amount of space made him appear even bigger. He occupied the majority of the bench seat, leaving me just a small portion. If he'd have scooted to the left even a mere inch, I would've been forced to sit in his lap. And with the smug look on the bastard's face, he knew it too. Hell, he probably was even wishing it.

I tried my best to keep my focus on the world zipping by outside the window, but with his demanding presence it was hard to concentrate.

Dean hustled ahead and opened the large wooden doors with ease, holding the door open while Baylor and Eden entered. Being the jerkoff that he was, he let the door go a split second before I started to enter and ran in, leaving me to force the door open on my own. It wasn't an easy task; where Dean made it look menial, it jerked me forward with force as it slammed shut on my ass.

If the day was any indication on how my stay in Oregon would play out, I couldn't wait to get back to Nashville. I grumbled under my breath as I stomped off towards the table where Eden and Baylor were already being seated. Dean was in the middle of taking off his black coat when I finally approached.

And I really didn't want to admit it to myself, and sure as shit wouldn't admit it out loud, but he looked amazing.

Almost edible.

Too bad his manners were shit and he was a fucking douche. He had on a pair of dark-washed jeans and a thick army-green sweater, the sleeves of which he immediately pushed up to his elbows. Even in the dead of winter his skin was tanned on his exposed forearms. My heartbeat faltered when I finally looked up into his eyes and a smirk played on his lips. I knew he caught me checking him out and he wanted me to know it.

Well, two could definitely play this game, and I could almost bet that I played it better. I was ready to wipe that cocky grin right off of his face.

I slowly and meticulously shoved the large buttons on my double-breasted pea coat through the slots, revealing my clothing underneath. Arching my back and protruding out my breasts, I slid the coat down the back of my arms until I caught the collar in my hands. I hung it over the back of my chair and then pulled it out to finally take a seat. I glanced up at Dean and saw his sights zeroed in on my chest once again and it was now my turn to flash a smug grin.

"Dean, did you check out there for a minute?" Eden pulled him from his trance, snapping his attention to her and making my moment of gloating end prematurely.

"Yeah, sorry." He hurried and took his seat, almost fidgeting as if he was out of his element. "Hey, how about a drink?" he asked then immediately raised his hand to alert the waitress.

I finally took a moment to look around the Tavern. It had an extremely homey feel about the place. And with the exposed beams and the all-around architecture, I could tell why Baylor enjoyed going there so much. Directly in front of our table was a small platform stage with only two steps leading up to it. I had to chuckle to myself, remembering Eden telling me about the time she sang karaoke and Baylor was there to witness it.

"Hey, guys," a feminine voice pulled me from my perusal and Eden's back stiffened in her seat at the sound. Looking towards the brunette I was immediately taken aback. She wore entirely too much makeup and tried to pull off the intense volume on her hair. It made her look cheap with a pile of frizz. An insult to her hair stylist.

There was absolutely no doubt in my mind that this was Maisie, Tillie's worthless granddaughter. Eden had caught me up on all things about Cottage Grove and this tramp had tried to get her talons in every eligible bachelor within thirty miles. If I wasn't mistaken, even Baylor was close to hooking up with her. A shiver ran down my spine at the thought. Good thing he refrained, his dick may not look the same after sticking it in *that* hole.

Maisie's eyes were locked on Dean's and you could see the lust seeping from her pores. It was tacky, really. *Rein that shit in, woman!*

"Ahem," I bellowed while clearing my throat. "Are you here to gawk at the man or take our orders?" Baylor immediately started coughing and Eden kicked my foot under the table. Dean, on the other hand, just stared right at me as if he was actually shocked that came out of my mouth. If I could fist bump myself, I totally would.

Maisie squared back her shoulders, snatched a pen from her apron and raised her pad towards her face. "Dean, what can I get ya?"

"We'll take a couple pitchers of Bud Light, Mais, thanks."

She started to walk away, completely ignoring me. The others may be all right with beer, but I sure as hell wasn't. "Excuse me?" I stated flatly. "I would actually like a margarita on the rocks and two shots of tequila with lime." I lifted my manicured hand and indicated the number two just in case she had difficulty understanding.

That earned me another eye roll from her as she turned around and stormed behind the bar.

Dean's glare turned icily towards me. "Rude much?"

Pretending to be hurt as if I actually gave a shit, I rested my hand against my chest. "Me? She was devouring you instead of taking our orders. By all means if you want to contract some ridiculous disease that has no cure from that one," I pointed in the direction she disappeared to, "then don't let us stop you. But she needs to do it on her own time or at least send someone over who is competent to take our orders."

Eden snickered at me, "Oh, Julia, I missed you and your attitude so much!" She threw her arms around me and I returned her hug. Eden was the only one who knew the real me, the one person who I allowed into my deeply guarded heart. Dean wouldn't get the satisfaction of knowing my tender side, there was no use.

"Why?" He sneered. "Eden, I don't get it, you and Julia are two completely different people. But yet, you're the best of friends. You aren't a bitch to anyone unless it is completely warranted. On the other hand, Julia exudes bitchiness. Are you really such a cold-hearted bitch?" He spat my way with venom and authority as if it would affect me. My steel armored heart threatened to crack but I kept my mask firmly in place. I used to be a woman who wore her feelings on her sleeve, but that woman was gone. Long gone. Now, it was often said that I didn't have feelings.

Shrugging my shoulder nonchalantly, "What you see is what you get. I don't sugarcoat things. Call me what you want if it'll help you sleep at night, I've been called worse."

Four empty glasses were placed on the table in front of us, along with the pitchers of beer. Maisie then placed my two shots and my margarita in front of me along with a plate of limes. I looked up at her and flashed a smile and sweetly said, "Thank you." See, I could be nice.

She said nothing as she left us to it and I handed off one of the tequila shots to Eden. "You know, she probably spit in your drink," Eden chuckled as she leaned into me.

"More than likely," I retorted. Reaching towards the middle of the table, I snatched up the salt shaker and licked my hand right above my thumb and sprinkled a hefty amount over the wetness. Eden and I each took a slice of lime and clinked our shot glasses together. My tongue snaked out licking off all the salt from my flesh while my eyes connected with Dean's. He continued to stare unabashed as I placed the glass to my lips and quickly tipped my head back, letting the tequila slide down my throat, igniting a fire on its trail. The clear liquid warmed me up from the inside and I finished by biting into the crisp piece of citrus. The way Dean's eyes flared and his corded forearms flexed told me everything that I needed to know and exactly what I expected. The man couldn't cover up his obvious attraction to me. I unnerved him, this much was true, but he definitely liked what he saw.

I grabbed my margarita and quickly gulped it down within two swallows. I needed to feel something other than just wanting to grab him by his face and fuck his mouth.

After another round of drinks I felt myself loosening up, I was having fun. Nowhere near drunk, but I was feeling rather tipsy. I tried my best not to look at Dean and I certainly hadn't talked to him anymore.

It startled me when Dean rose from the table and turned towards me, "Do you want another round?" Craning my neck up at his large frame from my place at the table I simply nodded. A lump formed in my throat. Christ, but the man was beautiful. If only he could keep his mouth shut. "I'm going to go grab another pitcher."

Watching his retreating form as he moved towards the bar, Eden bumped into my shoulder and pleaded in a whisper, "I know you don't really like Dean, but please play nice...for me."

"Well, if you give me no choice. But I make no promises. If he says some douchy remark, I can't be held responsible for what comes flying out of my mouth." She knew I was lying through my teeth but didn't press on.

A few minutes later Dean came back to the table, placing my margarita in front of me along with our shots. He sat down a stack of napkins and the top one caught my attention, or rather what was written on it.

It was Maisie's name along with a telephone number enclosed in a heart. I couldn't hold it in and busted out in a full blown laugh. Everyone looked at me as if I had just stated that I was a man.

"I'm sorry," I waved a hand in front of my face. Then sat the napkin in front of Dean. "*Maisie* wants you to call her."

Another smug look crossed his face and it made me wonder if he had any other expressions in his repertoire. "How about that, got her number without even trying. This must be my lucky night." He smiled triumphantly and carefully folded the napkin and shoved it into his pocket. I wanted to vomit.

"*Riiiight.*"

He leaned closer to me, invading my space, making me inhale his strong cologne which made my knees wobble a bit underneath the table. "You know, I think you're just jealous. Jealous because it seems people here are immune to your charms and bullshit. You come off as some spoiled little rich bitch who dresses like Sally Streetwalker and thinks she always has to get her way. Well, look around, sweetheart, you aren't in Kansas anymore. I don't think you'll be getting any men to eat out of the palm of your hand here."

I leaned in even closer, making our faces only mere inches apart and sneered. "Is that a challenge? You think you *know* me? If there is one thing to know about me is that I *never* back down from a challenge. What you see is what you get. You think because you got a number from the town whore that makes you somebody? Please, I could get a measly number in my fucking sleep."

Chapter 6

Dean

Her eyes turned menacing and I knew that I had severely pissed her off. It wasn't necessarily my intention, but the woman knew how to push me to the edge. I was just barely teetering on the brink of losing my sanity. I could've cared less that I got Maisie's number, she's a frigging slut, but I didn't make that little fact known. It bothered Julia and so I just pushed her further until her breaking point.

She scooted back from her chair and brought the shot glass full of tequila to her lips and swallowed, slamming the empty container back on the table. My pants tightened under the table at the vivid picture she painted with her lips wrapped around the glass; I knew that later I'd be picturing them around *other things*. She huffed and started walking towards the stage.

Karaoke had started about thirty minutes ago and the bar was filling up rather quickly. Apparently she knew exactly what she was doing, because she went straight to the computer that was set up with the karaoke equipment and began clicking around until a song started blaring out through the speakers.

"Is she drunk?" I asked, finally looking towards Eden who had a death glare of her own plastered to her face.

"Great, Dean. You're an asshole you know that?" Eden groaned, throwing a hand up in exasperation.

My eyes bulged and I was utterly flabbergasted. I replied, "ME?!"

"In order to be drunk you have to let your guard down and she doesn't even let hers slip. She doesn't get drunk, she gets angry, and then she gets even. You've done it now, I hope you're ready to reap the consequences." Her brows knitted together with anger. I didn't like pissing Eden off. Now that I was made to feel two feet tall, I picked up my glass and quickly downed the rest of my beer, needing to feel the effects from the alcohol streaming through my system more than it currently was.

Julia started singing "Masterpiece" by Jessie J and I literally almost swallowed my tongue. She may not have been drunk, but she was definitely feeling the after effects of the liquor. Something that Julia said stood out to me. *What you see is what you get.* Even though she could come across as inebriated, there wasn't a doubt in my mind that she would still be doing this very thing stone cold sober.

It amazed me how I could have such a hard-on for someone who could give the Antichrist a run for his money. I sat back with my arms crossed over my chest and just listened to the words of the song. She was stating that she wasn't perfect, that she was continuing to work on herself, but it was a major work in progress.

I glanced around the bar noticing all the men who had their eyes glued to her form, watching her like a beacon. I knew there was some truth to her song choice. It drew me in even more to the enigma that was Julia Caldwell.

Eden said that she never let her guard slip, but during this song I saw a glimpse. A peek of the lonely woman that she didn't want to portray. It made me want to get to know her, her true self. I wanted to peel away her resolve layer by layer and learn her innermost secrets. What made her the cynical woman that stood before me? I wanted to give her the benefit of the doubt, be the gentleman that I knew I was and see how she took it.

She completed the song and then shouted into the microphone, "Now, who wants to buy me a drink?" And added a naughty little wink at the end.

Oh yeah, she knew exactly what she was doing. She climbed down the stairs of the stage and marched directly towards the bar, swaying her hips seductively as she crossed the crowded room. She perched her ass in an empty seat and several guys followed after her like puppy dogs until they were crowding around her back.

I had an insurmountable need to ball my hands into fists underneath the table to try and calm my nerves from the very sight. A wave of jealousy hit me head-on and I wanted nothing more than to stalk over to her and throw her over my shoulder, caveman style, just to get her away from prying eyes. I had no right to pound on my chest like an errant caveman because men were fawning over her. She wasn't mine.

Fifteen minutes. That's how long I had to sit there watching various men dote over her, trying to flirt their way into her panties. Once she finally finagled herself away from her newfound suitors, she came sauntering back with a sly smirk on her face. She threw down what looked to be at least four different phone numbers onto the table in front of me and then took her seat with a satisfied smile.

Just as I was about to open my mouth, Ms. Tillie herself made her presence known at our table. Tillie had been the owner of the Tavern for as long as I could remember, her husband buying it for her before he passed. She was nearing eighty and chose to dress in very loud-colored velour pantsuits with bright red lipstick painted on her lips. She was a sweet little thing, often lending her ear to anyone who needed it.

"Eden, darling, I was hoping I would find you in here," she raved placing a wrinkled hand on Eden's shoulder. "I know you have so much going on with the wedding coming up this weekend, but I was hoping I could ask a favor of you?"

Julia's eyes lit up at Tillie's loud outfit; it seemed as if today's lucky color was the blinding chartreuse, and I could see the hint of a small smile playing on the edges of her lips. Tillie had that effect on everyone.

"Sure, what is it, Till?" Absolutely no hesitation was found in Eden's voice. She always tried to accommodate everyone. If you needed something from her, she would try her best to make it happen.

"Well, as you may know we have the annual auction being held here on Wednesday night and I was hoping you'd be the emcee?" Tillie glanced around the table with a twinkle in her eye, until she landed on Baylor; that's when she made a pout, protruding her bright red bottom lip out. "It won't be like it used to be with Baylor not in it, but we can count on you, right, Dean?" She glanced at me and smiled one of her brightest smiles which made her face crinkle at the edge of her eyes.

In all honesty I was hoping that I could get out of the auction, but it was great for the community, so I couldn't exactly turn it down.

"Yes, Ms. Tillie, I'll be here," I reluctantly agreed.

I could see Julia's brows crease out of my peripheral view, her interest piqued, "What sort of auction are we talking about here?"

Tillie wasted no time jumping into the details; she lived for this auction. "Every year we have the most eligible bachelors of Cottage Grove grace the stage to be auctioned off to the highest bidder," she leaned a little closer to Julia as if she was getting ready to inform her of a scandalous secret, her heavily glossed lips right at her ear and whispered, "for a date."

Her eyes immediately widened and this time Julia's brows almost disappeared into her hairline, "What is this, 1983?"

Tillie placed a hand on Julia's shoulder and gave it a gentle squeeze, "I know it seems a little archaic and no doubt a bit sexist, but it brings in quite a bit of money that we put back into the community. It's all in good fun. And even though Baylor won't be up for bid this year, a bunch of the ladies I play pinochle with are ready to get their hands on Cottage Grove's sexy new divorce lawyer." I felt my face heat up as Tillie looked at me and blew a kiss my way.

Julia threw her head back and released a sound that I felt all the way to my dick. "Oh my God! I have to see this," she slammed her open palm down on the table before pointing her forefinger at Tillie, "I am definitely there."

"I'll be there too," Baylor's brother, Bentley Jenkins chose this moment to interrupt as he crouched down in between Julia and myself. He extended his hand and Julia reluctantly grasped it. He quickly flicked his wrist and placed a lingering kiss on the back of her hand before showing off his trademark smile. "I do hope you'll be bidding." I saw a fire ignite in Julia's eyes at Bentley's unmistakable charm. He ranked up there pretty high with Maisie in the competition to be the town whore. And even though Julia was almost seven years his senior, Bentley wasn't opposed to getting with cougars.

Come to think of it, Julia was older than me as well. And *I* sure as shit wasn't turned off.

"Bentley, keep it in your pants, you charmer," Tillie joked. "So will you do it?"

Eden couldn't really refuse. I was surprised to see her hesitate for a brief moment before giving in. If anything, she would be needing the distraction in the next few days. Perhaps it would keep her stress level in check and her pre-wedding freak-outs to a minimum. One could only hope.

It was finally Wednesday and as much of a pussy as it made me, I was ready to see Julia again. The girls were gone most of Tuesday shopping or whatever it was they do and didn't get home until late. Baylor and I were each indulging in a beer and watching an action movie on TV when they came bounding in the door giggling over some nonsense. Once Julia's eyes connected with mine, her laughter ceased immediately and she quickly came up with the excuse that she was tired and all but rushed off to her bedroom.

I didn't have any clients that week, but I found myself at the office just for something to do. Otherwise my mind would stray to thoughts of Julia. As much as she got under my skin, I came to the conclusion that I wanted her. So there I was walking around Tillie's trying to make small talk with folks from the town, one eye never straying from the door so I could get a glimpse of Julia as soon as she walked in.

Tillie's was almost packed to the max and there was a police officer stationed at the entrance, making sure they were still under capacity. I had come straight from the office and was more than ready for a drink to quiet my brain, but I fought my way through the crowd first to try and locate Baylor and Eden. And if I was being honest, I was anticipating the thrill of going head to head with Julia.

After a bit of walking around, I felt eyes on me and I turned around to find Julia in my direct line of vision. How I had missed her entrance, I didn't know, but seeing her standing before me was utterly breathtaking. My heart rate increased, much as it always did in her presence, and I felt my palms begin to sweat. Many thoughts raced through my mind at the very sight of her.

I wanted to go to her.

I wanted to drag her down into the darkest part of the hallway and devour her.

I wanted to make her mine.

If only we didn't hate each other.

Chapter 7

Julia

Eden had told me earlier in the week that this benefit event was on the semi-formal side, so I couldn't wait to bring out one of my party dresses that I had packed, hoping for an occasion such as this. If Dean thought that the tame outfit of jeans and a simple top that I had worn to Tillie's made me a Sally Streetwalker, I couldn't wait to see what he would say about what I was wearing this time.

I meticulously scanned the room checking out everyone in attendance. All of the men were in suits, but none of them piqued my interest. Much to my chagrin, my gaze instantly honed in on Dean as soon as we arrived. He was wearing a sleek, fitted grey suit, with a crisp white shirt underneath, and a simple black tie. He exuded authority with his elegant movements and dominated the room with his tall frame. To me, he was the epitome of sex, it was just too bad he completely killed the mood whenever he opened his mouth.

I took off my coat, revealing my kelly-green long-sleeved lace dress, and placed it on the back of the chair at the table Baylor indicated was ours. When you looked at me from the front, you would think my dress was extremely conservative in taste. But lord almighty, when I turned around, the back was virtually nonexistent. This dress made me feel bold and confident, and if I dared to disclose, even a bit sexy. The material gathered at my shoulders before exposing the other ninety-five percent of my back, stopping at the curve of my ass. My hair was pulled in a side bun with curly tendrils flowing along the side of my face. I was completely in my element.

Holding onto my second glass of champagne, I walked around and idly chatted with a few people who Eden introduced me to. All while my gaze never strayed from Dean for too long. He was spending his time mingling around the room and openly flirting with every woman in attendance. Everyone except me...I didn't even get the satisfaction of a smart ass comment. I didn't know why it bothered me so much that he hadn't been paying attention to me, but it did.

Eden announced that the festivities were to begin within the next ten minutes or so and for everyone to get their money ready. That was my cue to hit up the ladies room, seeing how the champagne was going straight through me.

While I was minding my own business in the stall, I overheard two women barge in, stopping at the sinks.

"So, Miri, are you going to be bidding on Bentley?" Lady number one asked, her voice a bit distorted but sounding oddly familiar. I imagined she was probably reapplying her lipstick.

"Don't be ridiculous, Maisie." Oh, so it was the slutbag. I didn't know why the thought of her being there had never crossed my mind. Maybe perhaps because it was a bit above her class. "I'm not going to *buy* a date from him."

"Miri, you have been pathetically in love with him for I don't know how long, and here is your chance to actually do something about it."

"Bentley Jenkins has never noticed me, and I don't feel comfortable *buying* a date with him." Finally, someone on my level. When Tillie first explained to me about the auction, I couldn't exactly wrap my head around it.

"Well, I'm going to be bidding on Dean." My head perked up a bit more and I found myself leaning closer towards the door to hear their voices more clearly. Even though it wasn't news that the whore had the hots for Dean, it was different hearing it straight from the horse's mouth. I

More Than A Fling

was going to have to hurry up and make my presence known, but I wanted to eavesdrop a bit more. Sue me, I was a hair stylist after all, gossip filled my life. "Now that Baylor is getting hitched, Dean is the next best thing in Cottage Grove. Doesn't hurt that he's a lawyer and more than likely loaded."

"Seriously, Maisie? You can be such a wanker sometimes." I didn't know this Miri chick, but I instantly took a liking to her. She had serious spunk and a helluva pair of brass balls to straight up tell Maisie that she was basically being a bitch.

I had had enough of listening to Maisie's crap and it seemed like Miri had as well, I hurried up and flushed the toilet and yanked the door open on the stall as I nonchalantly walked towards the sinks to wash my hands. I tried my best to ignore the two ladies and keep my bitchiness to myself, but the slutbag had to go running her mouth.

"Oh, it's *you*..." She narrowed her eyes and spat in my direction.

I finally looked up from the sink and saw a blush creep up Miri's cheeks, no doubt appalled at Maisie, which I would certainly be. Then I noticed Maisie and she just looked utterly disgraceful and had a lip curled up in disgust. The bodice of her little black dress was a little too tight and her cheap red lipstick was covering the majority of one of her front teeth. Evidently she hadn't seen herself in the mirror, otherwise her expression wouldn't have been directed at me.

"Ah yes, Maisie, is it?" I did my best to come across polite, but inside I was ready to claw her eyes out. "I'm Julia, Eden's best friend from Nashville." Reaching around the dumb bitch, I grabbed a towel from the dispenser and began drying my hands. As I was throwing the crumpled towel into the trash, I looked directly into Maisie's eyes and said, "May the highest bidder win. Enjoy your evening, ladies."

I couldn't help but to lightly chuckle to myself as I went back to my seat, which was next to Baylor. There were so many different scenarios playing out in my head about how the situation could've been handled, and

I think the way it went down was a little too nice on my part. Growing up in New York, my parents put their money to use making sure I knew how to be prim and proper and that I was always polite to everyone I encountered.

Well, Mommy Dearest, look at me now, I know I've made you so proud.

Baylor leaned into me, "What caused that smile on your face?"

"Oh, nothing, nothing at all." I wasn't planning on bidding this evening, but I'd decided that it would be fun showing up Miss Nasty Pants. I settled back in my seat and crossed one leg over the other, eager to let the games begin.

Eden walked up onto the small stage followed by five guys, including Bentley and Dean. She raised the microphone to her lips and began the evening. "Good evening everyone!! Thank you so much for joining us here tonight!" She was always so full of life and could command the attention of everyone in the room without even trying. "Ms. Tillie has held this auction for the past twenty-five years. All the money always goes towards helping out the community of Cottage Grove and this year is no different. It has been announced that all of the proceeds will go to the new public library. I believe they've already broken ground for the new building, but tonight will help put in a more extensive children's section, so don't be stingy with your bidding." She pointed her forefinger towards all of the ladies in the audience.

Even though this was mostly a ladies' function, the men were given the opportunity to strictly donate an amount of their choosing. Or they could wait until the end of the date auction for other items that were donated from around the community to be auctioned off. I believe Eden told me that Baylor always put in a gift certificate for plumbing service and even Dean donated a divorce consult. Given my 0 for 2 batting average, maybe I should bid on that.

My eyes stayed glued to the stage, just willing Dean to look my way. It was as if he could hear me, because in the next moment his eyes landed on mine. His deep brown irises flared as they took in my bare crossed legs that were peeking out from underneath the table. I sat up a little straighter knowing he approved.

As Eden introduced the first two gentlemen, they each walked up while a different snippet of music played. The first guy was a short, rotund man in his forties who was on the verge of going completely bald, and was introduced as the local dentist. He reminded me of Ernie, as in Bert and Ernie. He stood stock still on the stage, not so much as even a blink came from him. His embarrassment was incredibly evident as his cheeks flushed and you could just make out the briefest hint of his sweaty armpits. But that could be due to the heat that exuded from the house lights that were pointed directly on him, right? He was a *real* catch.

His final bid was $50.

I think one of Tillie's pinochle friends took pity on him. Perhaps she needed some dental work and thought she would get a discount.

By the time it was Bentley's turn, the ladies were on the edge of their seats, their chops salivating just waiting to see who would get to nab the town playboy. "Bump and Grind" by R. Kelly began playing and you heard several women gasp before shouting off random dollar amounts, all before Eden even opened the bidding. Bentley swiveled his hips to the beat and seeing his seductive movements even had me feeling a little flustered.

Had this turned into a strip club and I wasn't made aware of it?

At any moment I was bracing myself to see Bentley's suit jacket come flying at the audience from off the stage.

Jesus, was it hot in here? I had to fan myself with my open hand and thought that they should've handed out those cheap paper fans as you entered the building.

Bentley was gorgeous, his muscles flexing through his clothing, showing off all of his hard lines and planes.

Too bad he was such a flirt.

I saw Miri standing off to the side out of my peripheral vision and her cheeks were flushed. She unabashedly had a major thing for Bentley Jenkins.

I looked back up at the stage just as Eden started off the bidding at $50. I peered over to where Dean was standing, waiting on his turn, and his pointed glare was directed at me. Was he pissed that I was gawking at Bentley? Hm, Dean Parker showing a bit of jealousy, this could be very useful.

Eden was up to $500 by the time I began paying attention again, and Bentley had the cheesiest grin spread across his face. The highest amount ended up being $750, coming from a little old lady in the front row. Looked as if it was one of Ms. Tillie's girlfriends as they gave one another a high five. Those pinochle ladies were cleaning house.

He didn't seem to mind that the winner could've been his grandma, he was soaking up having the highest amount of money bid on him for the evening thus far.

Finally, it was Dean's turn and I waited with bated breath for Eden to start talking. "Billie Jean" by Michael Jackson started playing through the speakers and Dean began strutting up to the front of the stage. He unbuttoned the single button on his suit jacket and threw the sides back, showing off his slim and trim waist. I subconsciously bit my lip trying to stop from either busting out laughing or releasing a loud moan. It was insanely comical but at the same time, also sexy as hell. I found myself squeezing my legs together as Dean danced on stage.

"Dean Parker here was raised in Cottage Grove, only to leave after High School, returning earlier this year to take over Baxter's Law Firm, now being the only divorce lawyer in town. His gorgeous brown eyes and apparent sexy moves are not to be overlooked. Ladies, shall we start the bidding at $50?"

Maisie weaseled her way up front, cutting through the throng of women, throwing her hand in the air just as the opening bid amount slipped from Eden's lips.

I sat back in my seat, crossing my arms in front of my chest, trying to remain aloof as if I wasn't interested and heard several women shout out dollar amounts. As soon as Maisie yelled out a bid, she was immediately cast aside as a higher number would be hollered. I could tell by her pursed lips and narrowed eyes that she was getting pissed that she was constantly being outbid. As much as I wanted to continue reveling in her demise, I thought it would be as good a time as any to put the poor girl out of her misery. I found my hand raising as I yelled out, "One thousand dollars!"

An audible gasp came from Maisie's lips simultaneously as Dean's head jerked in my direction. I could feel everyone's stare on me as I just casually looked at my fingernails.

Damn, I was in dire need of a manicure.

"Twelve hundred dollars!" Maisie yelled, and I had to stifle back my giggle, because I highly doubted she even had that amount of money. I remained calm, not even flinching; she on the other hand was ready for a knock-down, drag out brawl.

A new little old lady, who was seated with Ms. Tillie and her friend who had bid on Bentley, rose out of her seat and hollered with her hands waving in the air, "Fifteen hundred dollars!"

Wow, it appeared that the good lawyer was a hot commodity here in Cottage Grove.

The room grew silent as Eden began, "Fifteen hundred going once. Fifteen hundred going twice."

I shot up my hand once again, yelling, "Five thousand dollars."

"Holy shit," Eden breathed into the microphone. Quickly recovering her surprise she announced, "Five thousand going once. Five thousand going twice." I peered around the room trying to size up if anyone were to be so bold as to bid against me, paying special attention to Maisie and giving her an extra added smirk. "SOLD," Eden pointed in my direction, "to Julia Caldwell for five flipping thousand dollars!" Her bewilderment at me actually bidding on Dean, the guy I was supposed to hate, was written all over her face. I knew I had some explaining to do.

The room began clapping as Dean walked backwards towards his former place on the stage, his apparent anger radiating off of him. *What the …?*

Baylor had his elbows on the table and he casually leaned over towards me, a hint of a smile playing on his lips. "You don't like him, eh? And to think…" he lowered his voice to just above a whisper, "you probably could've had him for free."

"I don't know what you're talking about," I tried to play it cool. "I was simply doing my good deed for the season, you know being Christmastime and all." I tried to wave him off. "I didn't want to have to make fun of him for some old woman being the highest bidder. Besides," shrugging a shoulder, "I overheard Maisie in the bathroom talking as if she was ready to spread her legs right here on the floor and beg him to have his babies." I paused for a moment, trying to find a way to finagle myself out of this without digging my hole even further. "I guess I was looking out for his penis." I stated bluntly. "So, you see I just simply saw it as my civic duty to save his penis from falling off from the gift that keeps on giving that he would've received from her."

*Double damn…*Even I didn't believe all that bullshit I just spouted off. I didn't bid on Dean because I actually wanted him, did I? My own form of jealousy getting in the way?

The auction finally ended and I looked up to find Dean jumping down from the stage and rapidly stalking in my direction. Instead of him being happy about me outbidding everyone and donating to an amazing cause, he had a murderous glare on his face.

"Oh shit," I heard Baylor mutter.

Oh shit was right. I quickly rose from my seat and ran up to him to try and defuse the situation. What started out as a silly prank and the evidence of my jealousy, ended up hurting him and I had no one to blame but myself for putting that thunderous look on his face. My chest ached for believing I hurt him.

He continued storming forward until we were nose to nose and I had no other choice but to walk backwards to avoid being run over.

His steps didn't falter until I was completely pressed flat up against the wall and his arms came up around me, boxing me in so I couldn't move. He gave me no option other than accepting the brutal tongue lashing that was about to be bestowed upon me.

Dean's chest was heaving up and down, his labored breathing matching my own, and his eyes were narrowed at me. "What the fuck kind of game are you getting at here?" He spat in my face through his clenched teeth. My heart was beating so fast in my chest that I swore he could hear it, hell, maybe even the entire room could hear it. I couldn't form a coherent thought as my eyes flicked from his lips back up to his eyes. He didn't skip a beat as he pushed his groin into me and it was clearly evident that this little encounter was turning him on. A loud moan managed to slip from my lips as his hard length pressed into my belly.

I hadn't ever been a fan of voyeurism, but I was practically ready to beg him to lift up my dress and fuck me right there, audience be damned.

"Are you finished being a bitch and trying to ward me off?" He gently brushed his nose across mine, "I promise you it'll be explosive." His breath skimmed my ear and just as I thought he was about to dip his head down and press his lips to mine, he took a step back, turned on his heels and began walking away from me, seemingly unaffected.

I allowed myself a split second to try and recover from my lapse in judgment. Then I immediately snapped out of my lust-filled haze, with my anger taking precedence. I marched my ass right after him, charging around the still-occupied tables and chairs. "Listen up here, asshole, it was all a bit of fun." He stopped dead in his tracks. "I have the money, it was for a good cause and it gave me a laugh to piss off Maisie." My voice was continuing to grow louder as my anger surged above the surface. "It's not like we are going to actually follow through with the date, don't flatter yourself." He paused for a brief moment, with his back still facing me, then he stormed off and out into the night.

Chapter 8

Julia

The day had finally arrived, my best friend was getting married. Although as we had gotten closer to the actual day, I had started to wonder where Eden's head was. She was utterly calm and cool about everything, just going with the flow and hardly getting worked up about anything. I, on the other hand was preparing myself for the other shoe to drop.

I took care of everything that I could, keeping all the stress away from Eden and Baylor and more geared towards me. But it wasn't the stress of wedding planning that was getting me all out of sorts. It was the fact that Dean Parker was now ignoring me. Even while I cut his hair late Thursday afternoon, he wouldn't talk to me or answer any questions I asked him. He wouldn't even give me the pleasure of seeing his eyes trying to inconspicuously steal a glance in my direction. As much as I loved the thrill of the banter that took place between us, giving me the cold shoulder just made me want to wring his neck. How dare he brush me off, especially after getting me so hot and bothered at the auction?

Friday morning I found myself rushing into Cottage Grove Massage Specialists in order to get a Groomsman gift for Bentley. Baylor had already secured two tickets to a concert that Dean wanted to go to during the summer months, but completely forgot about his own brother. I came to the rescue with the idea of getting him a gift certificate for a massage. Even with the perplexed look both Eden and Baylor gave me, I knew it was the perfect thing for him. And once I walked into the lobby of the spa, it was like God was giving me a sign that this was exactly what Bentley needed.

Perched behind the counter, with one hand bracing up her chin as her eyes scanned across her Kindle, was none other than Miri from the auction.

Fate. It had to have been. Now, I wouldn't say that I necessarily believed in fate for myself; exhibit a and b being my ex-husbands, but it seemed the stars could be aligning for Miri and Bentley.

"Miri, right?" I spoke, startling her from her spot in her book. "I'm sorry, didn't mean for you to lose your place. I'm Julia, we didn't really get the proper introduction the other night at the auction."

She stared blankly at me before it dawned on her that I was the one in the bathroom. "Oh yes, sorry about all that. Maisie can be a...what's the word?"

"Bitch," I finished for her. It was true, plain and simple.

"Yeah, thanks," she breathed a sigh of relief most likely knowing that she could be so forthcoming with me. "She's my cousin and I know that I'm supposed to love her unconditionally and all that hoopla, but she gets on my ever-loving nerves. I was surprised that she didn't try to bid on Bentley just to rub it in my face. But she was for sure she'd win the date with Dean. Congratulations, by the way."

With the way Dean was being a dick towards me, I immediately dismissed it. "So, I'm here to purchase a gift certificate for an hour massage." I wasn't going to come out and say that it was for Bentley. I didn't even know if he knew she worked here, or if he even knew who she was, for that matter. But this could end up playing into the little plan that I was devising.

"Sure, no problem."

I could tell by the faint blush on her cheeks that she was pretty shy and reserved. Complete one-eighty from what I'd seen of Bentley.

"So, Miri, are you a licensed Massage Therapist?"

"I am. We are just slow at this time of the day, so I come up here to read and to wait on any customers." This would work out splendidly. Not only would Bentley come here to redeem his gift certificate, but there could be a likely chance that Miri would have her opportunity to touch her longtime crush.

Therapeutically, of course.

I wrapped up our conversation along with my purchase and invited her to the wedding before I took off.

Snapping out of my little haze, I realized that it was time for me to get back to work. I had been running ragged since early in the morning, trying to make sure everything was set up in the hall for the reception that would take place after the ceremony, so I had decided to hide out and take a little break.

I was nestled away at the end of a long corridor in the church, just trying to get away from everything and to get my head back on track.

"Julia!" I heard a man's voice hollering my name and coming closer to where I was hiding away. And then suddenly Bentley appeared in front of me, a huge smile forming on his lips. The man truly was beautiful. As fast as his smile appeared it was quickly replaced with a grim line. "Eden needs you, she's freaking out. I've never seen her this way before."

And that was my cue.

I knew her meltdown would happen sooner or later. I just hoped like hell it wasn't so bad that she would mess up her already gorgeously styled hair.

I took a deep breath, then quickly released it and said, "Come on."

As we retreated back down the hallway to the room where Eden was tucked away, we came across Dean, who eyed us suspiciously.

"Hey Deano! What's shaking? Had to go have a quickie with Jules, you know how it is."

"What the fuck?" I yelled, not believing Bentley just said that, and to Dean no less. Dean's glare was murderous once again, but this time it was directed towards Bentley. At least he'd branched out from his cocky smirk. I was desperately grasping at straws trying to find the positivity in this situation, not sure there really was any, though.

Bentley's arm wrapped around my torso as he dragged me along to Eden's room. "Come along, Jules, no use denying it. And don't act like you didn't love it." I was beginning to wonder if Baylor would miss not having a younger brother around. My morbid brain was already coming up with so many various ways in which I could kill him; slowly torturing him was becoming the frontrunner. Once we were far enough out of earshot, he leaned into me and apologized, "I'm sorry. I couldn't let him know that Eden was freaking out or else he would tell Baylor. It was best this way."

"Oh yes, it was best for you to tell Dean, of all people, that you fucked me in the hallway. *Right*," I stated bluntly.

"Oh, Jules, don't be so bitter," he said in a condescending tone. "Besides, I may have helped you out a little in the Dean department. I see how you two look at one another. It's all good, girl."

"You have *got* to be kidding me." I stopped dead in my tracks. I couldn't be hearing him correctly. These past five minutes had to have all been a dream.

Bentley stopped once he noticed I wasn't keeping up with him. He braced his hands on his hips, then raised one arm over his shoulder, pointing in the direction we needed to be going. "No more stalling, Julia, Eden needs you."

Shit.

Bentley caught me off-guard, making me forget about my best friend who could very well be on the verge of a panic attack...or a severe massacre. Either way, I'd have her back, armed with a paper bag to calm her breathing, or a shovel and trash bag to bury the body and hide the evidence.

The last thing I expected to see when I opened the door to the nursery, aka Eden's dressing room, was the sight of her jumping up and down on the bed. Don't ask me why there was a bed in the nursery, but there was, a twin, shoved up against the far wall, but that's beside the point. She was already dressed in her custom-made white chiffon lace wedding dress, and it was floating around her as she bounced in the air. The bodice was made out of silk material, while white lace covered her collarbone and ran down her arms. She was laughing away as she jumped on the bed like a child as if she were a free spirit. Bette Richardt, Eden's mom, glanced at me nervously, not knowing how to calm her daughter.

This wasn't the *freak-out* that I was preparing for, but Bette knew just as well as I did that Eden was soon going to combust.

"Jules, get your ass up here." I was still dressed in my plaid buttoned-up shirt and leggings with only my makeup applied, so it wasn't as odd for me to join in on the jumping as it was for her.

I threw off my shoes and lifted myself onto the bed, one leg at a time, and slowly started bouncing on the balls on my feet, barely lifting off of the bedding. I would hardly consider myself a spring chicken, but I got up there and followed Eden's actions with ease.

"Isn't this fun?" Eden asked, her breath running ragged due to her prolonged exertion. One moment she was laughing, having the biggest smile, and the next she started sobbing uncontrollably.

And the walls came tumbling down.

She flopped down on the twin bed, her dress poufing out around her. "I don't think I can do it. I don't think I can marry Baylor." Her tears streamed relentlessly down her face.

I looked over to Bentley, whose face instantly paled once Eden stated those words. Even though he lived in his brother's shadow, the love he had for Baylor was clearly evident.

I held my hand up to Bentley in a calming manner, I had to make sure that he knew this little blip stayed amongst the four of us. My eyes silently conveyed what I didn't need to bring out into the open. Not until he nodded his head in affirmation did I turn back to my best friend.

Really, she was more than my bestie, though, much more. She was my only family, my life.

Gently grasping both of her hands in mine, I brought them into my lap. Busying myself by slowly rubbing my fingers along hers in a soothing way, in a low voice I asked, "What brought this on? You love Baylor."

In between sobs she was finally able to speak. "I do love Baylor, more than anything. I'm just scared of how our future will unfold. I don't want to end up divorced and all alone like you."

I flinched, but didn't miss a beat while continuing to rub her arm. Even though I came across as not giving much of a shit, I wasn't entirely immune to her stab in the chest. I released a calming breath, trying to force myself to remember that she needed to get this all out in the open. Beside me her mother let out a shocked gasp and I knew she was on the verge of berating her thirty-three year old daughter. I shook my head, silently asking her not to bother because even though t hurt, ultimately Eden was right.

"Babe, there is a huge difference between you and Baylor and me and my ex-husbands. Baylor would move heaven and earth to make sure you're happy. You two have a love that 'm not ashamed to admit that I'm even jealous of." Her eyes continued to search mine as I told her the absolute truth. "You've loved him for over fifteen years, there is no doubt in my mind that you two have what it takes to make it for the long haul."

She released a long, drawn-out sigh that had my body relaxing. "You're right."

"Of course I am," I teased before releasing her hands and bending down to retrieve her discarded shoes. Something on the bottom sole of her satin heel caught my attention and a smile flittered across my face. This just further proved my point that they were completely, 100% meant for each other. He knew just what she needed even before she did.

"This just further reiterates my jealousy." I thrust the shoe in front of her so she could read the inscription written by her fiancé's hand.

You're my love, my life, my own personal Eden. I can't wait to seal the deal and make you my wife. I'll be the man in the tux down in front with the big smile on my face.

Love Always,

Baylor

She wiped one last remaining tear from her cheek as it slid its way down her skin, "I'm so sorry, Jules. I'm sure my face is all blotchy and my hair must be a mess."

"Yes...Yes it is," I replied, but with a smile on my face, not beating around the bush, "but lucky for you, I'm a professional." I winked at her then turned back around to Bentley. "I know people compare you to your brother, and since he's not here right now, I can say this." I thrust my forefinger in his direction. "With the heartfelt sentiment he just conveyed, you've got major shoes to fill. *Major*. To me, you're *way* hotter than Baylor," his cheeks actually turned a deep shade of red, which was a glorious sight. I made Bentley Jenkins blush and for some reason I didn't think that happened all too often. "I know you have your flirty and playboy ways, I'm not here to judge, but I hope you live up to the potential you possess and fall head over heels in love with someone." I spoke with such enthusiasm and determination that he had to know that this was nowhere near a joking matter. I was adamant about what I was conveying to him. "I hope you love her so fiercely that you don't want to know what it's like to spend one second of your life without her."

Towards the end of my mini rant, my voice began cracking at the conviction in what I was relaying to Bentley. Baylor Jenkins was a hard act to follow, but I knew that under Bentley's flirty exterior was a man just waiting for a woman to knock him on his ass.

He tried to brush off my little speech with a wave of his hand, thinking he was immune to falling in love Oh, it would happen to him all right, and when he least expected it, too.

It was now time for Eden to take my hand in her embrace, trying to console me, which made my breath hitch again. I looked down at our intertwined fingers as she gave me a soft squeeze. Bentley continued to stare at me, then he licked his lips and paused a brief moment before asking, "Have you ever had a love that strong Jules?"

Wasn't that the million dollar question? Did I even have the right to hope that I would find that type of love?

My heart panged in my chest, reminding me that I was still alive. I nodded my head, "At one time I thought I had, but it ended up being one-sided. But that's not something we need to rehash today." I released Eden's hand and stood from the bed. "Now come on, Bride, let's get your hair fixed and get you aisle-walking ready."

After I fixed the tendrils of hair that had loosened out of Eden's twist, I took my trusty can of aerosol hairspray and began over-obsessively dousing her hair.

Coughing from the fumes that I no longer noticed anymore, Eden sputtered, "You think that's enough?"

I shrugged a shoulder, and muttered honestly, "Just doing my part in the further destruction of the ozone layer. Also, I want to make sure that your hair isn't going anywhere today."

Chapter 9

Dean

Pacing.

That's what I was currently doing. Pacing back and forth along the carpet, more than likely wearing a path as I went. I couldn't get the image of Bentley and Julia hand in hand coming out from a deserted hallway out of my head. I was ready to go find him and rip him a new asshole. I wasn't used to dealing with this growing jealousy that festered inside of me.

It had been hard enough to keep away from her as it was. She'd constantly been trying to get my attention the past few days, but I thought it better for everyone involved if I tried to ignore her. I couldn't wrap my head around the kind of game she was playing the night of the auction, bidding on me as if it was a bit of fun. I could tell by our interaction afterwards that she had no qualms about expressing her attraction towards me, I just didn't know what her intentions were. Sure, I've been married and divorced two times but that doesn't mean it completely turned me off of love or women in general; I was a man, after all. Just when I put into my head that my job title was a hindrance to finding love, in strutted Julia Callaway. Did that mean that I wanted her for more than just a romp between the sheets? I hadn't the slightest idea, but the thought of her being with another man, that being Bentley, shook me to my core and downright pissed me off.

Anger wasn't an emotion that I often had and that seemed to be the recurring theme around Julia. I enjoyed making digs at her and wearing on her nerves, but her bidding on me at the auction, and five thousand dollars no less, shifted something inside of me, so I stayed away. Even while she was cutting my hair, flaunting her mouth-watering chest directly in my line of sight, I kept my distance. She knew what she was doing, trying to get a rise out of me and I almost couldn't keep my lust tampered down. But I suppressed my urge to fill both my palms full of her ass and thrust her onto my lap. It was hard as hell to act indifferent, but I did. I wasn't sure whether or not I wanted to push her completely away, but the scene that I had caught the ending to earlier told me that I had succeeded.

"Dude, would you seriously calm down? I'm the one getting married, it should be me pacing the floor," Baylor addressed, dissipating some of my anger.

"What? Sorry," I ceased my movements, trying to stand rooted in one place, but my legs were itching to pace again. That seemed to be when I did my best thinking, while I was stalking across the floor.

"Mind telling me what's got you pissed?"

I shoved my hands in the pockets of my tux and shrugged a shoulder. I couldn't fool him, no matter how hard I tried, and in my day that had been many a time. Baylor and I had been friends for well over half of our lives and it was virtually impossible to get anything past him.

"Are you upset that I'm marrying Eden?" He thought he was addressing the elephant in the room and a few months ago I would've actually said yes.

At that moment you could've tipped me over with a feather. Evidently I hadn't been as inconspicuous with my attraction to Eden as I had initially thought. With the three of us growing up together, we had formed a bond that I didn't think could've been broken until Eden walked away from both of us the day after graduation without a backwards glance. I often felt like the middleman having to constantly hear about Baylor's attraction to Eden and vice versa. It never occurred to either of them that I could have feelings for the girl as well. But like the dutiful friend that I was, I kept my feelings towards Eden bottled up inside. The thing was, I never would've acted on those feelings because that's not what true friends did, but that didn't mean that I didn't find myself asking time and time again why it couldn't have been me instead of Baylor.

A few months before, when Eden first came back to Cottage Grove, I confronted her as to why I hadn't been good enough for her. I was feeling at an all-time low, having two failed marriages against me. If that wasn't a blow to a man's ego, then I didn't know what was. Somehow I had gotten it into my stupid brain that I wasn't cut out for all of this love shit, and that being a divorce lawyer hindered me from having a fully functional, successful relationship. But any remaining attraction that I had towards Eden completely dissipated the moment I laid eyes on Julia.

Releasing a breath, I stated, "Nah, man, I'm genuinely overjoyed for the both of you. The two of you are perfect for each other." And it wasn't a lie, I didn't know two better people who were a better match. "But I will tell you this, even though you are my brother from another mother, if you hurt her you will have to answer to me." I lifted my mouth in a small smile and turned to have a seat in a nearby chair, "No, a completely different woman has me tied up in knots."

He followed suit, sitting down in the chair beside mine. "This wouldn't have anything to do with Julia, would it?"

I leaned forward, bracing my elbows on my knees, "I don't know what the hell is going on. We are constantly at each other's throats, and what's more, I enjoy it. I thought...I thought something might have been there, especially when she responded to me so desperately after the little stunt she pulled at the auction. But I must've imagined it, because your brother blatantly confirmed them hooking up in the hallway about fifteen minutes ago." I supposed Bentley Jenkins had met his equal in Julia, and I had always thought that *Maisie* was a slut.

"Listen, I don't know what the hell went on between her and Bentley, but what happened at the auction wasn't what you think. She tried to cover it up when explaining it to me, but I saw it in her eyes. She was jealous of Maisie. She said that she caught her in the bathroom bragging that she was going to nail you. I think in some twisted Julia fashion that was her way of protecting you from the crazy bitch that is Maisie and not being able to hide her jealousy while doing so."

Julia, jealous? I didn't know how to wrap my brain around this new information. But did it change anything?

"Here I am being a pussy needing the comforting today, when it should be you. How're you holding up, man?"

"Better than I thought I would be. When you know, you know. Eden has always been it for me, even though I let Kristina and her controlling ways cloud my judgment."

Wasn't that the truth? Kristina was Baylor's first wife and the mother of his daughter, Norah. Truths had come to light a few months earlier when Eden returned for our fifteen year high school reunion, revealing that it was Kristina who had made Eden run away all those years ago. I knew Baylor didn't regret his time with the bitch Kristina, because otherwise he wouldn't have my niece, but he missed out on a lot of time with Eden because of her.

The door flew open and I quickly looked up to reveal Bentley sauntering inside, a gloating smirk playing on his lips. I was ready to knock that stupid grin right off his face. "YOU!" I ground out between my clenched teeth, my jaw set to complete stone. I jerked my body up off of the chair and stalked his way, my anger growing more and more the closer to him I got.

He immediately threw his hands up in front of him, in a surrendering manner. "Hey man, what's got you so hostile?" He had yet to wipe that smirk off his face, not even letting it slip when he saw how pissed off I was.

Baylor calmly protested from behind me, "Guys, today is not the day for this."

"Well, then your fucking brother should have thought of that before he went sticking his dick in Julia. And in a hallway? No wonder she's so fucking cynical and comes off as such a bitch all the time, she deserves more than a fucking wall!" My voice was growing residually louder the more I talked. At this rate, I would be at a full blown yell and everyone in the church would be able to hear me. And what was more, I really didn't care.

I was now standing directly in front of Bentley and he shoved his hands in his pockets, still not showing any ounce of remorse or fear. Growing up with Baylor meant growing up with Bentley as well, he's younger than us by four years so he was constantly a pest. We had beat him up for fun back in high school, but in the present day he was unaffected.

"Are you done yet?" he asked nonchalantly.

"Am I done?" I grabbed him by the lapels of his tux and jerked his body towards me. Being 6'5" had its advantages, but with Bentley's size, he could've easily taken me. He wasn't fighting back which made me wonder what the hell he was getting at. "I'm just beginning, you stupid prick."

"You're welcome," he muttered, sounding pretty damn proud of himself and revealing just a hint of his habitual smirk.

I flinched, "I don't recall thanking you."

"If you would put me down, then I could explain things a bit easier." I complied to his request, albeit a bit reluctantly.

"You better start talking, NOW!"

He readjusted the jacket of his tux, making sure all of the wrinkles were smoothed out before he started on his explanation. "You see, you *should* be thanking me. I made you realize your feelings for Julia even if you didn't want to admit them to yourself."

I curled my hands into a fist, ready to punch him in his smug face. "I already knew what my feelings were for Julia."

"Well, then I helped you voice them out loud. I didn't have sex with her, although I don't know if I would exactly pass up the chance if it were to become available to me."

That was the last straw, my rage was creeping its way to the surface. I took a step forward again in his direction, reared my arm back and punched him square in his face, knocking his ass back a few feet. "She isn't a fucking object to be toyed with, she's a human being!" He started laughing as he covered his face with his hands and the knuckles on my right hand throbbed as I shook them out.

Baylor had already stepped in front of me to stop this nonsense, but I looked around him and spat out, "What the fuck are you laughing for?"

His laughter didn't subside for what seemed like minutes; he took his hand away from his nose only to see blood staining his hands. Then he pointed a finger in my direction as he looked up towards the ceiling, "I'll give you that one, Dean, but next time I won't just sit back and let it happen. You're already deeper than you think you are, and this little exchange is proof." On that note he turned on his heel and went in search of the nearest bathroom.

Shit!

I ran my hands through my unruly hair, trying to get a grip on the entire situation. What the hell just happened?

Chapter 10

Dean

Finally, I was able to get ahold of myself and settle my nerves and it was just in time for me to take my place next to Baylor at the altar. I knew I needed to apologize to the little Jenkins, but damn if it wouldn't hurt my pride to do so. I followed Baylor through the side door to the chapel and sidled up in between the two brothers. Quickly glancing to my left, I jerked my chin in Bentley's direction, silently conveying my inaudible apology. He nodded his head in return, acknowledging my plea.

The pianist began playing the wedding march and the doors to the back of the chapel opened. Two of Baylor's cousin's kids came forward, one with a basket overflowing with flower petals and the other with a satin pillow. Norah followed closely behind them, whispering instructions to make sure they stayed on course. Once her gaze reached mine, she beamed brightly while I winked in her direction.

I loved Norah as if she were my own and I was so thankful that she'd finally have the mother figure she deserved.

A moment later, my eyes focused on Julia like a beacon in the night. For a split second I actually forgot how to breathe. My palms began to sweat and my heartbeat sped up in rapid succession. She was utterly breathtaking in a crimson dress that stopped mid-thigh, with wine-stained lips. All the while she traveled down the aisle, she wouldn't look in my direction. It seemed as if the smart aleck was back and she was turning the tables on me, ignoring me. I supposed that turnabout was fair play and all that, but I didn't like not being on the receiving end of her gaze.

The ceremony went off without a hitch, Eden made a beautiful bride. Even after going through two weddings of my own, envy reared its ugly head. What I wouldn't give to have a love as powerful and effortless as the two of them had. Neither one of my marriages made me feel as if I couldn't go on without them. Being without Kate came close, but we wouldn't dwell on that part of my past.

Just taking in all the details and aspects of the reception hall, I could tell that Julia genuinely outdid herself in all of the preparations. Everything pulled together nicely and it had an elegant atmosphere. She made sure that everything was perfect for her best friend. Even though Julia didn't let many people into her heavily guarded heart, I could tell that she would ultimately do anything for Eden.

Glancing around, I could tell that the Mr. and Mrs. had yet to make their debut appearance and while the space was quickly filling up, I continued to scan the area for Julia and Norah.

I didn't expect to find them both sidled up next to each other taking residence at the candy bar. Pulling my hand from my pocket, I casually made my way just as Norah glanced back at me.

"Uncle Dean, look at all this candy." I could tell she was barely able to wrap her brain around all the different varieties. "Julia let me set most of it up and put me in charge of refills." The reflection in her eyes told me that she was thrilled to be given some level of responsibility for the evening. It made her feel important. She skipped off towards her friends on the other side of the room and I turned to face Julia, my features softening and a grin forming on my lips.

"Don't you look at me like that," she tried to sound offended, but there was a certain playfulness in her tone. "I do know how to act like a human being, contrary to popular belief." She let a small grin slip; I had yet to see a full smile reach her eyes. I was afraid that if I were to ever be on the receiving end of one of her mega-watt smiles that I wouldn't be able to live to tell about it. I'd die from her beauty. "And besides," she shrugged a shoulder, "I had an ulterior motive. It kept her out of the way and hopefully I won't be as tempted to come stuff my face with chocolate every time I'd have to come refill the dishes." An even bigger playful smirk danced on her lips.

Something, or rather someone, caught her attention and she called Bentley over. He didn't hesitate, in fact he smugly placed himself between us. Just as I was getting a moment of civility between Julia and myself, he had to ruin it by being alive. *Fucking pest.*

I cautiously watched as she motioned him to bend over towards her and she gently placed her hands on his cheeks. A burst of red hot anger radiated through my veins because the playboy was getting the softer side of Julia. Right then, I was torn between feeling remorse for punching him in the face, because of the aftercare he was receiving and wishing I had done something a helluva lot worse.

"I can't believe someone slammed a door on your face." She continued rubbing her finger alongside his nose. "You're going to have a nice shiner come morning, but at least the makeup worked well for the pictures." He pulled out of her embrace and turned towards me with a lifted brow. I couldn't believe he actually lied to her on my account.

"You know, accidents happen." He shrugged but not before adding emphasis to the word, *accident*.

I silently dared him to rat me out. I seemed to like it a little too much when Julia was a little hellcat.

She placed her hands on her hips bringing my attention to her tiny waist. "Are you sure it was an accident? It wasn't some past conquest you pissed off? You know hell hath no fury like a woman scorned and all that jazz."

"Nah, all my women know the deal upfront." He gloated like a major asshole. Bentley raised his head and looked off into the distance and his signature grin illuminated his entire face. The grin he normally reserved for when he wanted a woman to drop her panties.

I followed in his line of sight and saw that the goofy grin was directed at his brother Baylor and his new bride, Eden.

They each looked so happy and a pang of jealousy hit me square in the chest. Would I ever get the chance to look that happy?

I married Sophie during our sophomore year of College on a whim. And five weeks later, I had that marriage annulled.

Giving the simplest of explanations, she was fucking crazy. After we were married by the justice of the peace, I eagerly moved her into my place. It was as if a switch flipped inside her and she became a completely different woman.

But I supposed I did owe my career choice to her. I changed from litigation law over to wanting to practice divorce law. The idea of helping defend all the people (male or female) who jumped into a marriage, like me, and were instantly railroaded with a different personality, appealed to me.

It was an insane reason to switch up what path of law I studied, but I loved my job and what was even better was that I was damn good at it.

Then there was Kate, my second train wreck. Things were different with her. I took my time getting to know her and made sure that we lived with each other before we ever said I do. I thought we were happy, thought she was my forever. If only she had felt the same way...

Dinner and cutting the cake went by smoothly, but after my little trip down memory lane, my mood majorly downshifted. Plastering on a fake smile was the best that I could do at this point.

The attention of everyone in the room was focused on the middle of the dance floor, where Eden and Baylor were clutched in an intimate embrace, swaying back and forth, dancing to their first song.

Julia came up from behind me and huffed as she sat down to my right. Her brow was wrinkled and she had a perturbed expression marring her face. She was cute as hell when she was agitated. I wanted to ruffle her feathers a bit more.

"What's got your panties all in a bunch?"

Her gaze snapped to mine and she narrowed her eyes. I now knew all too well what the term 'if looks could kill' meant.

"Stuff it, asshole." She took a moment to ponder something, then a smirk formed on her lips. "Oh, and for the record, I'm not wearing any panties." She raised an eyebrow as if she was silently saying *top that*.

I could feel all of my blood hastily moving south, straight to my dick. Images of me jerking her to the nearest closet to challenge her on her admission ransacked my brain. I had to quickly think of something else to show that I wasn't all that affected by her words. Throwing up my hands in a mock surrender, I wanted to laugh at how easy I could rile her up, but I suppressed it because she could just as easily fire back another image that would further cloud my mind. No more blood needed to be shed tonight, and if I continued to press the issue that's exactly what would happen. "You're the one who came over here in a tizzy."

She began fiddling with one of the lit cream-colored votive candles that were sporadically placed on the navy blue tablecloths. She was running her finger across the tip of the flame, lost in the moment. Her mind was on something and it killed me to not know what it was. How could I help her if I didn't know what she was obviously stressing about?

Bentley came up behind her and placed two shot glasses down before her along with a salt shaker and a plate of limes. I was thoroughly surprised that he hadn't run off with some chick yet, but I guess it was still early in the evening.

I jerked up and quickly moved the candle out of her arms' reach. Being so close to the highly flammable alcohol wasn't the greatest idea.

"I thought you could use a drink, Jules. I could tell you were tense from all the way across the room."

It utterly grated my nerves that Bentley could call her Jules. Or maybe it just pissed me off that she hadn't offered me to use the nickname. Not that I could say that I would actually use it, her name is Julia. I didn't see a more perfect name for a stunning woman, other than possibly, *mine*.

"I can't believe she gave in to Baylor about their first song," she grumbled before throwing her head back and letting the cool clear liquid slide down her throat.

The expanse of her neck was now in my direct line of vision and I wanted to travel along the base of her neck to the tip of her ear with my tongue.

I was salivating for a taste of her.

"So that's what's got you in an uproar? The fact that he wanted "God Gave Me You" by Blake Shelton?" I would never understand women and I didn't even know why I bothered trying.

She slammed the empty glass upside down on the table and bit out between clenched teeth. "The first song is *everything*. Eden doesn't like country music, she works for a radio station that plays today's hit music for crying out loud. The first song should reflect both the bride and groom. So yeah, I'm in an *uproar*," she mocked.

Tightening my lips into a thin line I wanted to probe into the subject but I also wanted to keep my balls intact. My curiosity ended up winning. "Never pictured you as a girl who would care all that much about a first dance song. You superstitious about it or something?"

The way her eyes widened made me believe that I hit the nail on the head. "What songs were playing at your wedding?" I pressed.

"For my first?" A fearful expression slipped over her face before she carefully arranged her mask back in place; if you weren't directly looking at her right then, you might have missed it. Was there a possibility that she was afraid of her first husband? I desperately wanted to know. She began turning the empty shot glass around within her fingers, "Nothing played for our first song, but it should've been "Highway to Hell." She released a drawn-out resigned sigh, "I was a stupid young girl who made stupid decisions back then." With that statement I knew that there was some depth to the pain she felt but so desperately tried to hide.

"I wouldn't ever call you stupid, Jules," Bentley said, placing a hand on her shoulder.

"Oh yeah," she raised a brow, "Asshole and Dickhead are both a reflection of how stupid I could be."

Wow, that escalated quickly.

This conversation was vastly morphing into dangerous territory. She threw back the second shot and I glanced at Bentley trying to silently convey that we needed to change the topic of conversation.

The bride and groom's slow dance ended and an upbeat song was on queue immediately afterwards. Here was my chance to get close to Julia, hopefully without her biting my head off in the process.

"Would you like to dance with me?" I blurted out to Julia, the same exact moment Bentley did.

Fuck.

What were the odds?

"Gentlemen," Julia responded in a giggly tone. If I didn't know better I'd think she was walking a bit on the tipsy side. How many drinks had

74

she consumed? "The line forms to my left." She definitely was feeling it if she was openly flirting with me.

"Nonsense, Jules," Bentley said while reaching for her arm and prying her from her seat. "We can all go out and have a good time, even Baylor and Eden are getting down on the dance floor."

Julia perked up quite a bit after hearing that knowledge and seemed to snap out of her self-imposed pity party. She regained her composure and began walking towards her best friend and threw back over her shoulder, "You pussies coming or what?" Bentley looked to me with a quizzical raised brow, so I shrugged my shoulders, shoved my hands in my pockets, and followed along into the throngs of dancing bodies.

After a few songs I was in serious need of a break; it wasn't everyday this old man got down on the dancefloor. But since Julia was laughing and smiling and seeming to enjoy herself, I was going to tough it out. Norah even came up beside us and started dancing with her friends. There were now women with discarded shoes, hiking up their dresses so they could move a bit more freely, and men with their ties now decorating their heads instead of around their necks. Beer bottles and plastic cups were thrust into the air as several people sang to the songs.

A song began playing, which I learned was "Nobody Love" by Tori Kelly, but basically all hell broke loose. The women were cackling and carrying on about how much they loved this song. Julia was mouthing the words and swinging her hips to the beat, she looked sexy as hell. Her hair was beginning to fall out of its holder, leaving loose tendrils around her face and her body was coated with a sheen of sweat. She kept chancing glances at me at the same time that I was with her, and the briefest hint of a smile would play on her lips. She was definitely into me. I couldn't remember the last time that I enjoyed a wedding so much. This refresher was definitely welcomed to give me good memories of weddings and replace the bad of my own.

She glanced up again and looked directly behind me, "Be right back," she said to no one in particular and brushed past me.

Several moments later she came back within our group, holding hands with a younger woman. I knew her to be Tillie's other granddaughter, but I couldn't for the life of me remember her name.

"Miri, this is Dean Parker," she introduced us, and I gave her a slight smile. Then she spoke again, "Bentley, this is Miri Armstrong. Do you remember her from high school?" A faint pink blush rose on Miri's cheeks and it took Bentley a moment before recognition appeared on his face.

"Miri?" He questioned, before putting in place his famous panty-dropping grin, raising a brow, "My how you've grown into a beautiful woman." What was a faint pink staining her cheeks, now increased to ten different shades of red. Seemed as if even Miri Armstrong wasn't immune to Bentley's charms. She looked like a sweet girl, I hoped she knew what she was in for with him.

The songs changed up and now "Sugar" by Maroon 5 was playing. Our group seemed to have started filtering off in pairs: Eden and Baylor together, Bentley and Miri, which left Julia and me. She was paired with me whether she liked it or not. I was way past the point of exhaustion and I could barely stand up straight let alone dance right, so I was going through my repertoire of old dance moves. After I pulled out the sprinkler, Julia threw her head back and laughed. A genuine, straight from her gut laugh that left me tingling in all the right places.

"I didn't think you were capable of a full-blown laugh, especially one that was directed at me," I knew I was pressing my luck, but I couldn't for the life of me filter my responses towards her. "I think I just made it my mission in life to make you laugh like that every chance I get."

Her eyes slightly narrowed but her smile remained in place. "Keep showing off those hideous old school dance moves and you'll have no problem getting me to laugh at you. You look ridiculous."

The upbeat song ended and I waited with bated breath, hoping that the next song on the lineup would be a slow one, my fingers longed to feel the silkiness of her skin under my touch. My silent prayers were answered and it was the perfect song. I would now and forever associate "Thinking Out Loud" by Ed Sheeran, with Julia.

I looked around, making sure Bentley wasn't going to come and try to steal her away, but he appeared to be rather cozy in an embrace with Miri as they danced along. So I jumped at the opportunity, took one of Julia's hands in mine, gathered my other hand at her waist and pulled her towards me, snapping the distance between us closed. She peered up at me through her thick, lined lashes with just a hint of a smile and together we swayed back and forth to the beat of the music.

"You're good at this," she said almost a bit sheepishly, making her seem as if she were a little bit shy. Of course I knew that to be a load of crap. Julia was a ball-buster, a no-nonsense woman, shy was not a word I would directly associate with her. The only logical reasoning I could gather about why she would come across as a bit reserved would be that she was feeling this too—whatever the hell was taking place between the two of us.

"I've done this a time or two, and if I remember correctly, so have you." Bringing back a focus on both of our marriages, or rather, failed marriages wasn't a brilliant move on my part. But seeing how it was one actual thing that we had in common, I had to go with what I knew. Seeing a frown form on her face, wrinkling the space between her brows, I needed to quickly change the subject. We had only ever been bitter towards one another, but I had to give her a glimpse of what I saw in her, that I saw more to her than the never-ending banter. I cleared my throat, "You look beautiful today, Julia. I wanted to tell you that earlier, but I never found the right opportunity."

"You think I'm beautiful?" I didn't know if she was just fishing for compliments. With her being a straight chaser, I couldn't see her fishing for anything let alone caring what someone else thought of her. Perhaps she just wasn't used to getting true, honest compliments.

"I do."

"Did you really think I looked bad the other times?" she asked, wondering about the whole Sally Streetwalker comment. She looked gorgeous every time I've seen her. She pulled her lip between her teeth awaiting my response. I nodded my head yes, still remembering what she looked like every single time I've seen her, further increasing my need for her. My nostrils flared at the thought of us together, and then I breathlessly mumbled, "No."

"Are you trying to fish around for compliments, Jules?" I had to gauge her reaction.

Her face fell as she immediately dropped her arm from my shoulder, "It's Julia." She finished pulling away from me, albeit a bit disgruntled, and headed in the direction of the bathroom.

I didn't know what had transpired between us, but I couldn't let the entire moment pass us by. This was my chance to get her alone. I hoped like hell I didn't blow it.

I waited across from the door to the bathroom, my shoulder pressed up against the wall. So many questions were running through my mind, but the most pertinent was if I was making a big mistake by being here.

Life was full of unexpected chances, and you never knew if it'd be the right moment if you didn't face it head on.

Shoving my hands in my pockets, and leaning my back up against the wall, I tried to concentrate on something other than my building nerves. I then brought my arms behind my back and pressed my hands against the coolness of the concrete wall. As much as I tried to talk myself out of being there, I'd come too far to turn back now. I dragged my fingers along the ridges and grooves behind me and willed her to walk out of the bathroom door before I lost my nerve. Even though I was thirty-three years old, I felt as if I shouldn't be nervous to kiss a woman. But the thought of Julia turning me away and shoving my heart through a blender had my heartrate surging well above its normal pace.

The door swung out towards me, as my fingers pressed deeper into the wall. Julia emerged, her hair back in p ace and her lips stained with freshly applied lipstick. I almost wanted to apologize in advance for ruining her collected appearance. At last she finally looked up and acknowledged my presence with a lift of her brow.

She lowered her hands down to her sides and closed her eyes as she deeply inhaled air into her lungs. I didn't even let her fully exhale before I was off of the wall, wrapping both my hands around her waist and pushing her back against the cool concrete I had been occupying just seconds before. Her eyes flew open and not knowing what to expect, I held my breath to see what her reaction would be. The dilating of her pupils and the flicker of her eyes to my lips gave me all the approval I needed. I removed a hand from her waist and gently cupped her face. When she leaned into my touch, I knew I had her.

Closing in on the empty space between us, I began my descent to her mouth, but my curiosity was plaguing me on a question I had. Her breathing had picked up by that time and my further prolonging this interaction would no doubt get her blood boiling.

"Why does Bentley get to call you Jules, but I wasn't even awarded that luxury?"

"Because, Bentley doesn't irritate the shit out of me!" Her jaw clenched at my inquisition, which brought a slight smile to my face. I loved that I affected her so much.

Leaning towards her again, another question presented itself from something she mentioned to me earlier. How selfish would I be if I just kept my thoughts to myself, swirling around, never knowing whether or not I would find out the answer to such a pressing question?

This time I bypassed her lips, bringing my mouth to her ear, my breath caressing her outer shell. "Are you really not wearing any panties?"

When I brought my eyes back to hers, she tried her hardest to appear offended that I dared to whisper such a question.

The offense slid off her face and anger quickly replaced it.

I was so entranced with her reaction and those incandescent green irises that I never saw it coming.

The crack sounded first before the sting from her palm broke through on my cheek.

She slapped me.

She actually slapped me.

Nothing other than the pain radiating through my cheek registered at first. And before I could even lift my hand to my face, she had her hands curled around the lapels of my tux, much like how I had handled Bentley earlier. But instead of yelling in my face about my atrocious behavior, she surprised the hell out of me by slamming her lips to mine.

The surprise of her turning the tables on me quickly wore off as her tender lips melded to mine. A growl threatened to erupt from my chest as she casually coaxed her tongue along the seam of my lips, silently asking for access.

Didn't she know that she already had me? No permission was necessary to take what she wanted, what we both so desperately needed.

I plundered my tongue into her mouth as her arms wrapped around my neck. I allowed my right hand to move off of the wall and skim down her waist, starting from underneath her breast, all the way under her thigh until it was situated firmly within my grasp.

There were so many ways that I could describe what was happening, but the best was that it was feral and lethal, all rolled into one soul-gripping, earth-shattering kiss. This woman took just as good as she gave and had me completely under her spell with her kisses, so much so that I forgot that we were against a wall in a hallway, where anyone could see us. I didn't know what excited me more, that Julia was such a willing participant or the fact that we could be caught at any moment.

I hitched her thigh up around my hip, needing to get as close to Julia as I could. She immediately wrapped her other leg around my back, all while never breaking contact with my mouth.

Bracing my hand under her ass, I had to find out for myself if she was indeed walking around commando. I had to see if she would lie to me about something that was so menial, but entirely erotic.

Blindly trying to find the bottom edge of her dress, I finally succeeded, only to be halted by a layer of tulle. Why women would go to such extremes for frill and frou frou shit, when all it did was piss men off when we were in a hurry for some action or trying to prove a point, or in my case, both of the aforementioned.

At long last, I felt my fingertips reach the flesh of her bare thigh and the urge to fist bump the air for finding my treasure was strongly evident. It was as if I took so much time peeling the paper off of a present, with all of the ribbons and wrappings, but I wouldn't have the opportunity to look at my gift, yet...

I finally broke our kiss and focused on Julia's chest as she was trying to breathe air back into her lungs. The rapid rise and fall had me wanting to feast on her breasts as they were being thrust in my face. But with my hand still poised on her bare thigh, I had other things to attend to first.

Bringing my mouth back to her ear, I nipped on the flesh of her lobe before whispering huskily, "You won't confirm nor deny if you're wearing panties, so I'm going to find out for myself once and for all." I began my assault alternating nipping and sucking the expanse of skin below her ear. From the back of her throat, she released a sound so erotic that was a mixture between a yelp and a squeal. She loosened her hold around my neck and brought her hands to my shoulders, grasping onto them tightly to help brace herself.

I slowly began sliding my hand up her thigh so I could ultimately cup her bare ass. "Oh god," Julia panted, rubbing herself against me, trying to create some friction between her legs against my aching erection. Once I almost had reached my destination, a voice startled us out of our lust-filled hallway adventure.

Then I remembered that we were in a hallway, where anyone could find us.

"Well, well, well... Would you look at this," Fucking Bentley. I removed my hand from her bare skin and slowly started to allow Julia to slide down the wall. Careful of her regaining her footing and straightening out her dress.

A faint pink blush kissed her cheeks as she noticed my lips. She was completely focused on nothing other than my lips. Bringing her thumb up to my face, she swiped the pad along them, removing any and all evidence of our kiss.

She wouldn't look directly at me and wouldn't give Bentley the satisfaction of paying attention to him. As much as I was thrilled she wasn't feeding into Bentley's goading, I wanted to know what was running through her mind and I couldn't do that if she wouldn't look at me.

After cleaning off the smeared lipstick from my lips, she abruptly dropped her hand and she ducked out of the way, skirting past me to enter the restroom again.

My knees threatened to buckle, so I braced my hands against the concrete wall and rested my forehead against the cool ridges. I released a long, drawn-out sigh, trying to get my erection to subside, but the image of Julia panting and grinding against me would forever be seared into my brain.

"Way to embarrass her, asshole," I bit out between my grinding teeth, the tension building in my jaw.

"Me?" He pointed to himself. "You were the one who had her pushed up against the wall, mauling her neck for anyone to see. You're lucky it was me and not Norah."

Dammit, but he was right. I shoved myself up to my full height and turned to look at our peeping Tom.

His hands were shoved deep into his pockets and a smirk situated on his face. "Man, for two people who *claim* to hate one another, I'd really hate to witness what would transpire if you actually liked her." Then the bastard had the audacity to wink before he turned away. As he began to turn the corner to join the rest of the reception, he looked over his shoulder, "And here you were pissed at me for "taking" her in a hallway, what do you call this, *asshole*?"

Bentley Jenkins was officially the bane of my existence. Him and his smart ass remarks.

Chapter 11

Julia

I lazily pulled myself from out of bed, dragging my feet along the carpet heading towards the kitchen to get my daily dose of caffeine. I needed to feel the piping hot liquid warm my body from the inside out, waking me up so I could start my day. What was on the agenda would be a great question, but one I wouldn't have an answer for. I told Eden as she was leaving for her honeymoon that I most likely would be catching an earlier flight back to Nashville. But doing absolutely nothing all week had a certain appeal. I had nowhere to be, so I could binge watch whatever the hell I wanted to on Netflix and veg out in the process. But I would have to lay low in the confines of the house and hide away from Dean. What should be a simple task would prove to be anything but.

Exhibit A: He lived next door.

And 2: The kiss that took place last night seemed to be on a constant loop, replaying in my head. Like an old time movie, the reel playing over and over again until it all blurred together, where all you saw was lips on one another and his hand inching closer and closer to where I yearned for him.

Until Bentley had to ruin it all.

I dug around in Eden's cabinets, trying to find their coffee grounds. Surely they hadn't run out. Rummaging through the pantry, I pushed endless boxes of Pop-Tarts and bags of chips out of the way; they must seriously have a junk food addiction. I realized that I had completely rearranged the shelves of their pantry, but still came up empty handed as to where the damn coffee was stored.

Sliding onto a stool that was placed underneath the bar, I braced my head in my hands. How could I hide out of Dean's sight when I had to venture out to get coffee?

I'm sure he was on the edge of his seat with anticipation, just waiting for me to appear outside. And there was absolutely no way that I could mentally survive a full week without my caffeine pick-me-up. My whole day would be thrown off, and then I would be too moody to sit around all day and watch movies.

I could already feel the effects of not having my daily cup. It was becoming harder to concentrate and my mind was turning into a jumbled mess.

Could someone have a panic attack from not having any coffee?

Moving my face towards the counter, I rested my cheek against the cold granite and tried to keep my breathing composed. My thoughts finally strayed from my lack of coffee predicament and moved to much more dangerous territory.

Not only did I have an addiction to coffee, after the night before I could safely say that I had a strong addiction to Dean, and more specifically, his kisses.

Without realizing what I was doing, the pad of my fingers brushed across my lips, remembering the kiss down to the smallest intimate detail.

I'll admit that I was surprised to see him standing outside of the bathroom. But what caught me off guard even more was the fact that he actually took the initiative to kiss me.

And Jesus Christ, the look in his eyes right before he stalked towards me, the fierce determination, had me clenching with desire. I had to physically force myself to close my eyes in order to take a breath.

But it just wouldn't have been genuinely Dean if he didn't annoy the crap out of me and push me to the edge. He got me all worked up before he riled me up, so I did what any woman would've done: took matters into my own hands and shut him the hell up.

I couldn't pinpoint the last time I had enjoyed kissing someone so much. Anymore to me, it was a means to an end. Kissing for me, led to getting emotionally attached, so most of the time, when I hooked up with a man, I hardly ever offered my mouth. But with Dean, after the first touch, I craved more.

If Bentley hadn't interrupted us, I didn't know how far things would've gone. Being completely caught up in the moment, I was oblivious to the world around us. And when Bentley called us out, I had never been so embarrassed. I was chalking up the lapse in judgment to my brain being totally consumed and clouded by lust. And I allowed my head to hang in defeat while I retreated back to the restroom for hiding; normally I never ever looked down at the ground unless I was fixing my shoe. I always held my head high and accepted whatever judgment and remarks people cast my way and often did so without even blinking. My resting bitch face was perfected. But something about being caught wrapped up in Dean disturbed me. I didn't want onlookers gawking at something that should've been considered private.

This admission was extremely dangerous, especially to my guarded heart, which is why I needed to steer clear away from Dean Parker.

A loud rap on the front door caused me to jerk upright.

Could it be the coffee gods coming to help me out?

Did they deliver?

I didn't know why the thought of it being Dean never even crossed my mind. But once I unlocked the brass deadbolt and yanked the door towards me, allowing the frigid air to envelop my body, there he stood all of his delicious sexy glory.

I felt goosebumps break out all over my body and my nipples pebble underneath my t-shirt, reminding me that I was still in my pajamas and without a bra. My breath hitched in my chest at the sight of his smirk, then I took in every last inch of him, ending with his boots, which were heavily lined with snow.

Snow? What the?

Leaning to my side, I peered past Dean into the front yard and sure enough there appeared to be several inches, perhaps even feet of snow. When Baylor and Eden were leaving for the airport around midnight there had only been a few flurries. It must have come down hard to accumulate so much in the matter of a few hours.

My shoulders slumped in disappointment as I looked back up to Dean. His eyes were focused on my t-shirt, more specifically, my nipples. I quickly crossed my arms in front of my chest so he could detour his peering elsewhere.

"Can I help you?" I bit out rather sternly, my mixture of annoyance from the snow and lack of coffee made for an absence of a cheery disposition this early in the morning. As if an upbeat disposition could be associated with me on any given day.

He readjusted his knit cap on his head, pulling the edges down over his ears, "I just wanted to give you a heads up that many of the roads are closed due to all of the snow. Baylor had mentioned something about you might be wanting a flight out of here soon, but I don't think it'll be happening." He had the start of a grin forming on his mouth, the edges of his lips turning up, before he thought better of it and remained with a grim expression.

A defeated sigh passed between my parted lips, escalating my annoyance level. I was planning on staying the week through, but I didn't like the fact that I was now forced to stay without a way out. This would make my plan of hiding out that much more difficult to execute, especially when the person I wanted to be hiding out from was standing literally a foot in front of me. I wanted to slam the door, cutting off the cold air that was entering the house, but not before yanking Dean inside by the front of his coat. Surely there were things that we could partake in that would keep us warm and entertained.

"Well, I'll be next door in case you need anything," he started to turn around, accepting my silence as a dismissal and dammit if that didn't make me feel ten kinds of awful. My mother used to do the same thing to me and it hurt so badly. Sure, I loved the sparring that occurred between Dean and myself but the last thing I ever wanted to do was blatantly hurt him.

"Wait, Dean?" I said, my voice coming out small. He slowly turned around and I had to tighten my arms around my body just to try and block some of the air. What I really wanted to ask was if he would wrap me in his arms and keep me warm, but this wasn't exactly the time for it. So instead, I chickened out, and asked about my second desperation, "Do you know where in the world they keep their coffee stored?"

He let out a chuckle, "Check the freezer. Baylor has a thing about keeping it in there before he goes out of town. He probably didn't even think twice about doing it." And with that he turned back around and trekked through the snow, retreating in the path he made prior to coming over here. I looked around outside before finally closing the door and I noticed that not only did he make a path to come over here, he had shoveled the snow on the sidewalk as well.

My major bitch was out in full force today and I had to figure out how to fix it, but first I needed a cup of coffee, where the grounds *were* definitely stowed away securely in the freezer, and a shower. Now that I had time to really dwell on our interaction, he saw me sans makeup and in my pajamas. I definitely needed redemption for my appearance and actions, and I knew exactly where I was going to start.

Freshly showered, I blow-dried my hair before pulling it up in a loose knot on the top of my head. I knew that I wasn't going to be go out anywhere, but I didn't ever feel completely normal without some kind of makeup on, so I simply covered my face in pressed powder, lined my eyelids with black eyeliner and gave a few swipes of my mascara wand to my lashes. It wasn't my normal routine, but it would do for a lazy snow day.

It had been years since I'd had a snow day, so I was ready to take full advantage of it. But in order to get the ball rolling, I needed to go risk my chances out in the snow and head over to Dean's.

Outfitted in a pair of black leggings, Eden's rain boots, a red v-neck shirt, and a long, gray knit cardigan, I walked out of the house and ended up running all the way to Dean's porch once the frigid air hit me. I was so excited to extend an olive branch that I stupidly forgot my coat and I was paying the ultimate price by freezing my tits off.

I hurried up and jerked my hand up to his front door and pounded my knuckles repeatedly against the wood, conveying my urgency for him to hurry up. My teeth were starting to chatter and I had to perform a little dance in order to keep the heat flowing throughout my body.

"Hurry the hell up, Dean," I muttered to myself as my teeth clashed against one another. This brilliant peace offering was suddenly beginning to seem dumb. *What was taking him so long?* I knew he hadn't left, because there weren't any tire tracks and he even said the roads were closed.

At long last, I heard movement on the other side of the door and then he said something.

Did Dean have someone with him? Did he hook up with a woman after our scorching kiss? Oh my god, did I just interrupt him sexing up a woman?

Oh shit, maybe this entire trip over to his house was a bad idea, I couldn't feel my toes which had me further thinking this situation was whack. This was why I didn't let people in. They took advantage of you and left you even more messed up than how they found you.

He inched open the door and before his eyes connected with mine, I blurted out, "Is there someone in there with you?"

"What?" He asked looking to me with confusion before what I said dawned on him. "No, I'm on the phone with Bea," he held his phone away from his ear for a brief moment before ushering me in. It bothered me that he hadn't openly elaborated on who Bea was and I wanted to holler out at him in a fit of jealous rage, demanding he tell me who she was.

Damn all of these emotions for making themselves known. I'm supposed to remain indifferent and aloof when all I wanted to do was claw her eyes out. I'd barely been in Cottage Grove a week and already I wanted to put a hit on two different women.

As soon as I stepped inside his living room, he closed his door and resumed his conversation with 'Bea.' This left me to take in his house, his space.

While his décor was nothing to write home about, it was all tastefully done. At least there were no empty beer bottles or flattened pizza boxes piling up amongst the space.

A large khaki microfiber sectional took up most of his living room; an oversized matching ottoman was centered in the middle. Pushed up against the wall was a black entertainment stand that housed a big screen TV and that concluded his furniture. The only item he had hanging on his walls was a black framed mirror.

It was sparse and lacked major color, but oddly enough, I felt right at home.

Being that we were in the same room, it was hard not to eavesdrop. The gentleness in his tone towards her was my undoing. I wanted to be the one he called 'hon.'

"Make sure you keep warm, hon. If I'm able to get out later, I'll call and get a list of what you and Carl need. I'll talk to you later."

"Julia?" I snapped my attention to him, not fully realizing that he'd hung up with Bea.

"Huh?" I hesitated, my teeth still suffering the onslaught of chatter from the cold.

He finally took in my outfit and lack of a coat and quickly closed in the distance that remained between us. Placing his hands on my forearms, he briskly began rubbing his palms up and down my arms trying to bring me some warmth.

"Sweetheart, what did you come over here without a coat on for?" I stiffened at his term of endearment at the same time he paused his movements on my arms, as if he didn't intend to allow that word to slip from his lips. I relaxed in his embrace just as he resumed.

I let the term roll around in my head, and I decided that I liked being dubbed sweetheart more than hon.

He was still waiting on an answer and there I was mentally sticking my tongue out at Bea for getting the better nickname. "I didn't have your number."

His brows rose almost into his hairline, before a smirk formed on his face, "You want my number?"

"Ugh, don't flatter yourself!" I tried to make it seem that I wasn't as anxious to come over here as I was. I didn't need the fact that I found myself wanting him to go straight to his head, or in his case, more than likely, his dick. "I didn't even think about putting on a coat, and I certainly didn't think it'd take ten minutes for you to answer your door."

"I'm sorry, I was in my office talking to Bea, my secretary." Finally, an answer to who the mysterious Bea was. "Her and her husband are older and I wanted to make sure they were warm and had everything they needed." I seemed to melt even more into his embrace at the thought of him going out of his way to help his employee and her husband. I was beginning to like the softer side of Dean Parker, calling me sweetheart and being a Good Samaritan. "You still haven't told me why you're here, not that I mind it. *At all.*"

Oh, right, "I ran over to invite you to lunch, as sort of an apology for earlier. I'm a real bitch before I have my coffee," I finished with a shrug as if I wasn't a bitch all the time.

"Only before?" He retorted, while peering down at me and not being able to hold back a chuckle. He totally called me out on all my bitchiness. Had I really met my match?

"Yeah, you're so hilarious," lifting one of my hands, I brought it to his stomach and grabbed a chunk of skin through his shirt with my index finger and thumb and squeezed, pinching him hard. "Laugh it up, asshole."

"Ouch," he winced, "Julia, what the hell?" His hands dropped to his sides and I immediately regretted pinching him, because I missed his contact.

His hand came towards me and he captured my chin, tilting it back until I had no other choice but to look at him. Once I opened my eyes to his, the creases surrounding his eyes stood out and glancing down, I took note it was because he was smiling. That full-watt smile was for me. All for me. "Listen to me, never apologize for being who you are. You may have a level of wit about you that most don't know how to handle, but that's what I find most unique and alluring about you. Don't let your 'give a fuck' slip in order to apologize to anyone, especially me. If someone wants you or wants to be in your life, then they need to prove that they can handle it all. The good and the ugly, the bitchiness and the sweet side that I know is lurking around in there," he began searching my eyes, "I've seen glimpses of that sweet girl. Someone has done something to you forcing you to hide her, but I'm determined to bring her out again."

My throat constricted and it was becoming harder to swallow and I could feel the onslaught of tears beginning to build in the corners of my eyes. People didn't say things like that to me, they would quickly cast me aside as a selfish bitch and then be done with me. Was I that easy to read? Or was Dean just piecing together the glimpses that I'd given him? All in all it was way too much for me to handle at that moment. I was ready to haul ass back to Eden and Baylor's house and not come out the remainder of the time I was there.

"What's on the menu?" He snapped me from my trance and I almost forgot that I had invited him over for lunch.

"Oh, I figured since there was so much leftover baked chicken from the reception that I would put it to good use and make chicken pot pie."

"Do you like to cook?" He asked with his brows raised, genuinely surprised.

"I love to cook and I love to eat. Being that I do a lot of both, I'm hardcore into Zumba and Yoga." His eyes flared at my admission. I paused for a second before deciding to go ahead and let him into a part of my past. I voluntarily let layers of myself peel back, if he wanted the full on Julia experience, I was going to at least give him part. "My nanny taught me how to cook when I was little and I learned how to make the best pot pie dough from her. She used thyme in her recipe and it was absolutely amazing. I have some made up and it's resting in the fridge now."

"That was a little presumptuous of you making the dough beforehand. Did you think I was that much of a foregone conclusion?"

Giving him a slight shake of my head, I said, "No, but like I said, I like to eat. I'm sure it would've been gone in a few days with or without your company."

He loudly clapped his hands together and rubbed them back and forth, "Well then I think I need to taste this special chicken pot pie." He smiled one of those mega-watt smiles, that I wanted to say were reserved just for me, even though I'm sure it'd been used on his fair share of women, but I reciprocated anyways. I smiled so brightly, a true smile, it reached all the way to my eyes.

"Absolutely, come back over in about an hour." I started to retreat for the door, my smile still lingering on my lips.

"Wait," he placed a hand on my arm, halting me in place before rushing out of the living room and returning with a coat in his clutches. He held open the jacket at the collar for me to slip on, "Put this on before you step outside, I don't want you to get sick."

I left Dean's house seeing him in a whole new light. I never asked him to call me Jules because I loved the way Julia sounded coming off of his lips and I would rather he used my full name rather than a nickname. But when he called me sweetheart, a warmth surrounded me, and I decided that I liked him calling me that. He was such a good man, it was such a sweet thing for him to call and check up on his secretary. But I also loved that he wasn't afraid to go head to head in a little verbal sparring with me every now and again.

I believe that I had just left a little piece of my heart with him back at his house. I was officially falling for Dean Parker, and I couldn't entirely call it a good thing. Wrapping his coat tighter around my body, I smelled the coat just inside the zipper, inhaling his scent, rich with soap. I wanted that scent to surround me, but for the time being his coat would suffice.

When Dean came back over almost an hour later, I was elbow deep in flour and dough, trying to get the fickle mixture to cooperate. He took a seat at the bar, cradling his chin in his hands while his elbows rested on the countertop, taking in what I'm sure looked to be a giant mess. I cracked the rolling pin down on top of the smashed ball of dough, then grabbed both sides of the pin and began rolling it back and forth across the surface.

"You enjoy doing this?" He asked, flinging out his hand indicating the process of making dough from scratch.

"Oh yeah, it's very therapeutic!" I grinned as I smacked down the pin, releasing a loud 'Thwack!' "You see, the trick is not to handle it too much, if the dough gets too warm then it'll start to separate and break apart." I didn't know why I told him that, it wasn't like he really cared. But there he stayed, listening intently to my every word.

Once I got each of the two pieces of dough, one for the top and the other for the bottom, rolled out to the desired size, I rolled the bottom piece along the rolling pin and unfolded it into the round baking dish, and pressed the edges deep into the bottom.

"How about some wine and music?" Dean asked and he pushed himself up from the stool and once he saw my head perk up and nod, he retreated into the living room. A few seconds later I heard the sounds of a trumpet blaring through a speaker that was placed on top of one of the kitchen cabinets. And just with those first few notes I knew exactly what the song was.

A wave of nostalgia trickled through me, I remembered my daddy playing this song all the time when I was younger. Most of the time, it happened when my mother was out shopping or getting her hair done. She wasn't one to encourage any bit of fun in the house.

I had to wipe a stray tear away from my cheek and I hoped that Dean hadn't seen me, but the concerned expression on his face told me that he had. "This was one of my daddy's favorite songs when I was little. He loved Otis Redding period, but "Try A Little Tenderness" was his favorite."

The song was halfway finished and my absolute favorite part was coming up. Our eyes locked and my mouth quirked up in a grin. Dean began mouthing the words and tried to add a little soul to his movements. The second the song changed from a sensual rhythmed song, the beat picked up tempo with the drums, trumpet, and the sax, and Dean got all into it. He thrashed his head around, clutching his fists up to his face, and did a slow shake of his hips which immediately reminded me of John Cryer in *Pretty in Pink*. I couldn't hold back the laughter that spilled from my lips. Throwing my head back, I continued to laugh. Even though he was acting utterly ridiculous, he had never looked sexier to me. I found myself prancing around the kitchen right along with him.

"(Sitting On) The Dock of the Bay" came on afterwards and I couldn't help but sing along with the lyrics as Dean handed me a glass of wine. I spooned the pot pie mixture into the baking dish and once I had the top crust in place, I crimped the edges and poked slits along the top to allow steam to escape.

The finished pot pie was shoved into the oven and within forty-five minutes it'd be golden and bubbly. I couldn't wait.

"You have a pretty voice."

I felt my cheeks blush at his kind words. "Oh, thank you. My mother insisted upon enrolling me in singing lessons when I was four."

"Wow, so young?"

I pondered on just how much I should let him in. The past was just that, the past. It needed to stay there and rekindling ill-harbored suppressed memories wouldn't do me any good. Talking about my daddy and my nanny was one thing, but discussing my mother was a whole other ball game. I decided that a little insight wouldn't hurt.

"I grew up in Manhattan and I had two options, either take singing lessons or piano. My mother was adamant that I take piano just as all her friends' children were doing, so naturally I chose singing. I'm honestly not sure why she gave me the choice between the two because she was so hell bent on the fact that I'd made the wrong decision."

Chapter 12

Dean

She shrugged a shoulder before continuing on, "Maybe this was her way of giving me a test, seeing if I would be the dutiful child who followed her mother's every whim. Or perhaps my daddy actually stood up to the woman for once in his life." She had a faraway look in her eyes as if she was reliving a memory.

I didn't want to pry, but I was curious to know more about Julia. Anything and everything she would divulge. "Did you and your parents not get along?"

She promptly frowned, her brows creasing. For a moment, I almost thought she wasn't going to respond, that I'd gone too far, prying into things that I had no right to know, but she finally released a breath and said, "My daddy and I got along pretty well, even more so when my mother wasn't around, which was basically all the time. My dad has been gone for, gosh, twenty years now, I was fifteen." My heart hurt for her, for the things I was hearing. "My mother on the other hand, we have butted heads since the day I was born. Anything I could do to defy her, I did. Pretty sad when you were raised by your nanny and knew from the young age of three that your mother never wanted you." She shrugged her shoulder again and tried to force a small smile. She thought she could show me that it didn't bother her, but I could see her underlying hurt. Her eyes didn't conceal everything, when I looked into their depths I could see the scared child that she was, and then the anger from her father leaving her so early, and the animosity she so clearly had against her mother. She wasn't as great at hiding her pain as she thought she was. I bet she was shit at poker, because her face would reveal her cards.

"But I had my nanny, who I wouldn't trade for anything. She made my childhood worthwhile." She grabbed a dish sponge in her hands and began scrubbing the kitchen island free of the remaining flour and pie dough, I suspected to keep her hands busy. The only alternative was to fidget under my gaze. "The minute I turned eighteen, I packed my entire life into one suitcase and left." She glanced up to me, "Haven't talked to her since," then she began scrubbing once again. "Oh, she did try to take me to court once I turned twenty-three. Trying to come after my trust fund that my daddy had set me up with when I was born. She wasn't awarded anything but a dig to her pride and once I was given rights to the account, I haven't touched a dime that the trust contains." She paused for a moment then said something that shocked the hell out of me. "Well, until the auction last week."

I knew my mouth was held slightly agape, but hearing that she used money that she deemed untouchable stirred something deep inside of me. Putting her reservations aside for a great cause showed me that she had so much more to her than she wanted people to see. I fucking wanted this woman in my bed and more importantly, in my life. Taking a deep breath and slowly releasing it, I tried to slow my ass down. I was getting way ahead of myself. Sure, I could throw a few words her way, but with all the let-downs that had accumulated in her lifetime, what she really needed were actions.

Finally, she shook off her uneasiness, "What about your parents?"

Now it was my turn to feel ill at ease. I didn't want to further distress her regarding her upbringing by putting emphasis on mine. One thing that I hated was that I couldn't fix how people treated her in her past but I could focus on her future if she'd let me. Blocking out all of her unsatisfactory memories by replacing them with new ones. Memories that included laughter, sure, the occasional banter every now and again, and love.

Love.

Yeah, I wasn't going to dwell on that word just yet and I quickly had to school my expression to hide the anxiety that seeped into my veins with that one word. I had just gotten Julia to start opening up to me. Love was the last thing I needed to think about, but it had a way of creeping up in your thoughts and completely blindsiding you.

I cleared my throat, still wary of bringing up my joyous childhood in comparison to hers. "My parents still live together in Cottage Grove." Despite the bitter cold weather outside, I was getting rather warm within the kitchen. Having the heat and the oven on wasn't helping matters. "They've been married for thirty-five years. I'm an only child, but they've definitely had their work cut out for them through the years." I used my hand to indicate my entire body in which her eyes reluctantly followed. Nodding, "I mean they had me for a kid, I'm sure it wasn't all sunshine and roses for them, especially when I snuck out of my bedroom window on a regular basis." I tried to loosen her up a little regarding the situation, I needed her to crack another smile. No matter how small, I would still consider it a victory.

We fell into a comfortable silence, not really feeling the need to fill up space with idle chitchat. When she opened up the oven door to remove our lunch, all the aromas from the pot pie permeated through the air making the entire house smell of home-cooked comfort food.

My mouth began salivating when she sat a plate down in front of me at the bar. If this heaping helping tasted half as good as it looked and smelled, I may never let her go.

I scooped up a major forkful, making sure I got a little bit of everything in the mix, for the perfect bite. I brought the steaming fork towards my mouth and glanced up at Julia before taking the initial plunge. Her nervousness was vastly apparent as she had her bottom lip tucked in between her teeth and her brows were furrowed. She genuinely cared about my reaction to her cooking, which led me to believe that she allowed more things to get to her than what she let on.

She acted like she didn't care what people thought of her, and to some extent it may be true, but right then her self-doubt that she tried so hard to keep buried was creeping up and invading her thoughts.

My initial reaction to the taste would immediately give my thoughts away and I wanted her to perceive them as good even if I didn't find the dish to my liking. I didn't want her to end up being disappointed in herself. My worrying as well as hers ended up being all in vain. Once my perfect bite hit my tongue all the textures and flavors exploded on my tongue. The creaminess of the roux, the bite of the peas and carrots mixed along with the chicken, and the flakiness of her crust along with the subtle hint of thyme—I had certainly died and was sent straight into culinary heaven. This heaven far exceeded any of my expectations because it included Julia.

I was fairly certain my eyes rolled back into my head before I reluctantly came back to earth for another bite. Julia had eased up on gnawing at her bottom lip, but I realized she needed verbal confirmation. "This has to be the second best thing I have ever had in my mouth." I pointed the fork down towards the plate, "It's fucking amazing, Julia."

You could see the gears turning in her head, battling her curiosity, but a hint of a smile appeared on the corner of her mouth. I wanted to goad her to go ahead and ask the obvious question and soon enough her curiosity won. She quirked a brow, "And pray tell, what precedes my pot pie?"

A devilish smirk played on my mouth and in my mind I was rubbing my hands together, because she had caved in so beautifully. I placed my fork down beside my plate and rested my arm on the counter, leaning my torso in closer to her and whispered, "You."

Instant recognition hit her and I knew she was now transported back into the hallway of the wedding reception last night, where our tongues and mouths were ravaging one another as if we couldn't get enough.

It was the first time either of us had brought up the kiss and for a moment I was worried that I'd see a flash of regret in her eyes, instead I was awarded with the opposite. Her lips tipped up into a full-on brilliant smile which left her utterly gleaming.

"You should do that more often," I murmured as I shoved another forkful into my mouth.

Confused, she replied, "What do you mean?"

"Smile. I love it when you smile. Even your slight smile is beautiful, when your lips just barely lift, but when you really give it your all, it's majestic and absolutely breathtaking. You get these lines next to your eyes that crinkle and it makes you look radiant." My fingers were itching to touch her face, especially the aforementioned area.

And...now I've scared her away.

She turned away from me to dish up her own plate and a hushed silence fell over the room. I was certain that I'd said too much but a fleeting smile remained on her lips, reassuring me about my response.

Since she had slaved away on this glorious lunch, I insisted that I would clean up. It helped that I washed dishes like a boss. Eden and Baylor had the luxury of a dishwasher, while I did not, so a good old sponge and dish soap was my specialty. Julia had seen my house and knew that I was somewhat domesticated, not feeling the need to keep my house cluttered, and not that I needed to emphasize how great of a catch that I was, but that I could do chores without having to be nagged or goaded.

So I was elbow deep in soapy suds and hot water using a sponge to disintegrate any and all grimy food remnants. I briefly turned my head towards Julia, who was resting against the island behind me to my left, wielding a freshly topped - glass of wine. She took a small sip, looking at me over the top of her glass before dangling it from her fingertips down at her side, her eyes never leaving mine.

I glanced back at the plate I was rinsing off before bringing my gaze back to the blonde who was garnering my attention.

"You like me..." I posed it as a statement rather than a question, but I wouldn't expect anything less than a rebuttal from Julia.

She threw her head back and released a long laugh. The kind of laugh that makes it hard to breathe and no sound comes from your mouth. She thought my statement was hysterical; my confidence was quickly diminishing. It took her a bit to recover and if I ever had any qualms of self-doubt she brought them out front and center topped off with a neon flashing sign. "No, I *like* cool summer nights. I *like* chocolate frosting. I wouldn't say that what I feel towards you falls under the 'like' category. I'm slowly learning to tolerate you."

Tolerate me? I wanted to call her out on her bullshit, but I pressed on. "You're attracted to me, though, I could tell in the way your breath hitched at the auction and...well, in the way you mauled me at the wedding."

She placed her glass down on the bar, "Excuse me? Mauled you? What am I, a lioness out stalking her prey?" She began slinking her way towards me, slowly putting one foot in front of the other until she rested against the counter right next to me. I was able to watch all of her movements while I continued to slave away in the hot water. "Waiting in the dimly-lit bushes for the feeble gazelle to wander by before I strike and make my move?" I was the feeble gazelle? Oh, hell no, but I shrugged a shoulder. "You're ridiculous. I'll admit that there is a degree of attraction there, but that doesn't mean that I have to like you."

Chuckling, I counteracted, "But you *will* like me."

"Don't get your hopes up."

I'd have to admit that she was doing a splendid job trying to convince me otherwise, or maybe she was failing to convince herself. "In the meantime, I think we could have a bit of fun..." I couldn't believe that I was actually going through with this, but I needed to show her that despite our thrilling banter that we could be good for one another. "Of the naked and sweaty variety, that could perhaps at times take place between the sheets."

She eyed me warily, clearly sizing up whether my proposition was real or not, as I continued on with the dishes, finishing up the last of the silverware. After a minute, she pushed herself off the edge of the counter, standing up straight and readjusting her long, flowy cardigan, wrapping it around her torso and narrowing her eyes as if accepting my challenge.

Words, sweetheart, I need the words.

"What are you waiting for?"

Momentarily stunned, I didn't think I had heard her correctly but the raised brow she was sporting told me otherwise. I didn't let another moment pass or give her the chance to change her mind before I took one giant step in her direction, cradling her face in my wet hands and crashing my lips to hers. I felt the water and suds run down my arms, dripping onto the floor, but having dry hands wasn't a good enough reason to break our connection.

Moving a hand blindly until I reached her hairline, I loosened the knot that was securely fastened on top of her head, feeling the silkiness as her hair came tumbling down in waves, resting in the middle of her back. I thrust a hand into the thick strands, pulling back with just enough pressure so she'd be forced to break our connection and look into my eyes.

It elated me to no end that her breath was coming out in short pants and her eyes were glazed over with lust.

"Why'd you make me pull away?" Her voice came out as a deep rasp.

"I just wanted to be sure that you were certain about this." I was certain myself that I had lost my balls somewhere along the way. That was the only legitimate excuse I could conjure up that would explain why I was questioning her about this when she could very well be naked by now.

Without blinking, she responded, "Dean, I'm positive. Like you said, there is an attraction between us and I think a fling is the perfect way to get us out of each other's systems."

I visibly flinched without warning and couldn't help but feel that I'd been dealt a major blow to my gut. Of course this would be just a fling for her and nothing else. Well, no one could ever say that I didn't appreciate a challenge. It would be my distinct pleasure to open Julia's eyes to see how good we'd be together.

She wasted no extra time before she leapt into my arms and locked her legs behind my back before attacking my mouth once again. Forcing myself to shut off my brain and just be in the moment with her, I shifted her back off of the corner of the kitchen counter and began our retreat into her bedroom.

While Julia felt so absolutely fucking perfect in my arms, moving blindly around the house proved to be no easy feat. If I had said that I knew what direction we were headed in, it would've been a total lie. And my point was proven when I tumbled into a wall in the hallway. Julia's back slammed up against the wall and she released a slight whimper in the back of her throat and was close to biting my tongue.

"Shit, I'm sorry, sweetheart." There I'd let that word slip again, but I couldn't help but worry I'd hurt her.

Squinting up at me, "Perhaps you could let me finish this little journey out on my own feet."

I reluctantly sat her back down on the floor before picking her up again, this time with one of my hands braced behind her back, and the other under her knees, cradling her close to me.

"Where is the fun in that?" I joked.

"You're impossible." she ground out around a giggle. I would never grow tired of hearing that sound.

As I maneuvered our bodies the rest of the way to her room, I stuck my nose in her hair, inhaling the warm vanilla scent of her shampoo. My instinct was to close my eyes and relish in her smell, but the way she began clawing at my shirt told me she was wanting this as much as me.

I made sure her ass was firmly planted on the bed before I proceeded to peel her cardigan and t-shirt off of her arms and free her breasts from the confines of her bra.

Being somewhat of a boob man, I already knew that hers had been surgically enhanced, but I just wasn't prepared for the beautifully sculpted masterpieces that were right in front of me. I engulfed each breast with a hand and there was still plenty spilling out of my palms.

"I've wanted to do this since the first time I laid eyes on you," I breathed. Not able to wait for a response, I leaned forward and latched onto an erect nipple and swirled my tongue around. Her hands grabbed ahold of my hair and pulled, almost to the point of pain. Her breathing increased as I released one breast right before devouring the other.

Julia's hands began frantically clawing at the shirt on my back, desperate for contact. I eased up on my assault of her breasts before pulling my shirt up and off over my head. Her eyes widened at the sight of my torso before she raked her nails down the taut skin of my abdomen, forcing a hiss to expel from my lungs.

"Like what you see?" I smirked, her gaze still transfixed on the expanse of my chest.

"Eh," she slightly shrugged a shoulder before locking her eyes back on mine. "I've seen better." Instead of dwelling on her verbal dig like she would anticipate, I just let it fuel my fire.

I was about to rock her world so she wouldn't remember any other man she had been with. Game fucking on.

I braced a hand behind each of her knees before yanking her legs down the bed making her lay flat on her back for me. Shock registered on her face at my quick movements before I tucked my fingers under the edge of her leggings and panties, slowly bringing them both down her legs and off in one fell swoop until she was completely bared to me.

Prying her legs open I could see the glistening moisture of her desire on her core just begging for my attention. My resolve was wearing thin and I didn't know how much longer I could hold out before sinking balls deep into her.

She looked at me through her parted lashes as she gripped her own breasts, kneading her milky flesh, and a strangled, "Please," fell from her lips. She was pleading for my touch, how could I deny the softer side of Julia?

A swipe of my tongue along her slit was all it took for an inaudible cry to rip from her throat and her back to bow up off of the bed. My dick had never been so hard but that was the effect Julia had on me. Sucking her clit into my mouth, her hands grasped the linen sheets on the bed, yanking them towards her as she squeezed her eyes shut and shouted my name.

My own heart rate increased and I felt like I was on top of the world for eliciting the reactions from Julia that I was. One of my hands skimmed the apex of her thighs before I plunged two digits deep into her heat.

"Dean! Dean, baby I need you! I need you inside of me!" she screamed.

She certainly didn't have to tell me twice. I kissed her clit once more before removing my fingers. I grabbed my wallet from the back pocket of my jeans and quickly retrieved a condom, then proceeded to shuck my pants. I went to rip open our protection and she stunned me by snatching the package from my hands and placing a hand in the center of my chest in order to push my back down into the mattress.

Julia sucked her bottom lip into her mouth and bit down on the plump flesh as she flicked her eyes from mine down to my straining erection. The way she was looking at me with such intensity and raw hunger

I was afraid that all it would take for me to blow my load was a single brush of her fingertips on my cock.

My eyes snapped shut tightly and I held my breath as she rolled the condom down my shaft, securing it in place. Straddling my hips, she grasped the base of my cock and lifted herself up, hovering my tip at the entrance to her core. She idly stayed in this position, as she had all the power. One hand was now braced in the center of my chest as she slowly proceeded to press herself down on me.

Patience wasn't exactly one of my strong suits, especially when the end result was something I craved so desperately, so I lifted my hips up off the mattress, impaling her the remainder of the way until my cock was fully lodged deep inside her.

"Fuck," I strained through my gritted teeth. I had never felt something as incredible as it was to be deeply rooted inside Julia. Her slick warmth surrounding me, I could stay in this position forever and it still not be enough.

I finally let her have her bit of control once she finally started to move. Rising up off of my cock, almost to the point of pulling completely off of me, she thrust herself back down, impaling my cock into her pussy harder each time she repeated the action.

My hands were each spread out on her milky white thighs as I never strayed my gaze from her body, watching her take what she needed from me. I skimmed my fingertips up her torso, quickly ascending towards her breasts. Once I engulfed each into the palm of my hands, giving each a good firm squeeze, she gasped and threw her had back allowing the sensation to overcome her.

"Oh, yes," she breathed between pants, her head still tipped back as I continued to mercilessly assault her amazing breasts. Each time I would brush my thumb across her nipple, her breath would hitch and cause her to increase her speed.

With her head thrown back, the bottom of her hair was brushing against my upper thighs, sending the strangest tickling sensation to shoot directly to my balls.

The expanse of her neck was exposed and beckoning for my tongue. What kind of man would I be to not comply?

I used my arms to push myself into a sitting position, where our torsos were now flush with one another. Her thighs remaining on the outside of mine, me changing things up a bit didn't change her movements in the slightest. I wrapped one of my hands around the back of her neck while bringing her exposed throat towards my awaiting lips.

I felt first before hearing a growl rip from her throat as I licked a trail from the base all the way to the underside of her chin, simultaneously reaching my other hand around to grip her ass, giving the cheek a firm bite with my fingertips.

I roughly kissed her throat a few times knowing she was getting an extra sensation from the bite of the stubble on my face. I tilted her head down so I could search her lust-filled gaze with my own. We stayed that way, staring at one another for several moments, as I began feeling something shift inside of me. I wasn't anticipating to meet someone like Julia, but now that I had, I didn't want to let her go.

It was stupid of me to only offer a fling, but that was the only way to have her. I'd be craving a whole helluva lot more once she left.

You have a fucking gorgeous woman riding your dick as if she owned it and here you are ruining the moment by not being able to get out of your own head.

"Julia," I groaned as I shoved my fingers through the silky strands of her long, flowing blonde hair, her eyes never wavering from my own. Her eyebrows rose in an inquisitive manner as my mouth drew closer to hers. "You're so fucking beautiful," I muttered before closing the remaining distance between us, fusing our lips together.

108

Her arms moved to my shoulder to brace herself and her quicker movements. Once I felt the bite of her nails as they surged into my back and her pussy begin to clench around me, I knew she was close.

It was time for me to take over control.

Shoving my hands under her thighs, I quickly flipped her over onto her back beside me before I moved my body on top of hers.

The glare she was throwing me told me she was angry about the lost contact. She didn't need to worry because about ten seconds later, I slammed home into her and I wasn't going to stop until we both claimed exhaustion.

Thrust after relentless thrust, I continued until I felt her walls contract around me. I reached under her thigh to hitch it around my hip so I could really drive home.

"So fucking good," I ground out just as her nails scratched across my back and her walls tightened around my cock like a vise.

"Shitttt," she screamed as the wave of her orgasm hit her. "Dean!!!" The sound of my name rolling off of her tongue in the midst of her orgasm tipped me further over the edge to where I needed to be. My muscles tightened as what had to be the most mind-blowing orgasm I'd ever had ripped through me.

Sweat covered our intertwined bodies and after a few moments our heart rates returned back to normal as I slipped out of Julia's heat. I leaned down and pressed my lips to hers for a brief kiss before pulling away and seeing the satisfied smirk that played on her lips. I instantly missed the contact as I stood from her bed and retreated into the bathroom to clean up.

By the time I came back with a washcloth for Julia, she had already curled onto her side and was fast asleep.

I couldn't help but worry what would happen to my already fallen heart once she left Cottage Grove. *Could I talk her into staying?*

Chapter 13

Julia

My muscles screamed out in delicious agony as I shifted around on the bed, the sheet I was wrapped up in slowly drifted to my waist exposing my naked breasts. I couldn't remember the last time I felt so completely sated and I didn't want to peel my eyes open on the off chance I would shift from my relaxed state. I had never known pain to hurt so good, the ache consumed me in places I didn't even know existed. And the fact that I awoke with a ghost of a smile on my lips wasn't at all lost on me. My lashes fluttered against my cheek as my hand rose to my parted lips where they were bruised from being kissed raw. I had sex with Dean Parker; delicious, unabashed, scintillating sex and he was still alive to tell about it, and what was more, I loved it.

The plan was to stay as far away from him as I could, although since he lived next door it was going to be damn near impossible. But as the morning progressed, I found myself actually enjoying his company. Yeah, I just admitted that, but if you repeat those words to anyone I will DENY. DENY. DENY them to my grave. Even though sour memories were dredged up, the easy banter between the two of us more than made up for it.

I wouldn't ever forget the look of desire that had shown in his eyes before he forcefully threw the soap sponge in the sink. Recalling the fact that he didn't even take the time to wipe the suds off his arms before he slammed his mouth to mine almost made me come right then and there.

Sex had never been so much fun for me, it was always an itch that I needed scratched and often mechanical on my part. He made it all about me, even letting me take control for a bit, and brought out so many foreign emotions, most of which hit me like a thunder bolt that I didn't even begin to know how to conceal. And the orgasm that ripped through me, Oh My God. Yeah, I was pretty sure that the fire he ignited inside of me began to thaw bits and pieces of my frigid heart.

Finally, rubbing my eyes so I could attempt to get used to the brightness before I fully fluttered opened my eyes, I angled my arms above my head to get a good stretch. Loosen up those overworked muscles a bit. I was cautious to not bother Dean in case he was still asleep. *Did he even fall asleep?* I was so spent that I honestly didn't have a clue.

With my eyes fully opened, I glanced over to my left and to my dismay the remaining space in the bed was empty. *Had he left?* The sun continued to stream in around the drawn blinds alerting me that I hadn't slept very long. *Where'd he go?*

My insecurity was on the cusp of rearing its ugly head when Dean appeared in the doorway. He braced his forearm on the frame causing his shirt to lift up, revealing the ridges and contours of his stomach. My heart fluttered and my tongue involuntarily darted out to wet my lips as my eyes zeroed in on his bared skin. *Wait, why was he dressed?*

"Damn," he groaned causing my eyes to snap up to his, my brow lifted in question. My nipples puckered and my breath hitched at his hungered expression. He pushed himself from the door jamb and swiftly stalked towards me, dropping to his knees when he reached the edge of the bed right beside me.

His eyes skimmed down to my breasts before bringing them back to my face where they flared. "If I had one wish to make, it would be always being greeted by this sight. An exquisite woman baring her breasts to me while she lazily stretches from her sleep." His statement kicked up my heart rate and made my cheeks flush from his boldness.

His hand engulfed a breast and I arched to move myself closer in his direction. The surge of wetness between my legs told me I was primed and ready for rounds two through four.

"Dean," I whispered. "Fuck me, please." The plea fell from my lips so easily. I didn't know what came over me, I *never* begged. It was just unheard of. And yet, here I was and he had yet to say a word. Had I rendered him speechless?

His throat bobbed as he swallowed and the contemplation of my begging was clearly causing him inner turmoil. What was there to think about? A naked woman in front of you, ready and willing and you have to have a conversation with yourself on whether or not you want to do something about it? I thought that what had taken place between the two of us was phenomenal, but as more and more time passed I started to think that perhaps it was just me. His silence said everything that I needed to know. How could I have been so stupid? He released his hold on my breast and I scrambled to sit up and pulled the sheet up to my neck where it was now covering me completely. I clutched the thin material to my chest, although it wasn't the suit of armor that I preferred to be wearing when dealing with such an impactful blow.

My throat tightened as the first wave of unshed tears glistened in my eyes. It stung to be so openly rejected. Dean's brow furrowed and he released a groan as his head fell face down onto the mattress. His voice came out in a muffled whisper. "Dammit, Julia," he braced his open palms on the bed and pushed himself upright until his face was only centimeters away.

My bottom lip trembled while I forcibly blinked back my tears. I may act like a cold hearted bitch, but it didn't mean that I was immune to feeling emotion and the ache of not being wanted. What shocked me more was that I was so upset by Dean's refusal.

He lifted a hand towards my face and I flinched before his fingers ever made contact with my cheek. He searched deep into my eyes as if he was trying to find an answer but I wasn't even aware of what the question was. He seemed sad, full of regret.

The chips in my frozen heart that had begun to thaw before were well on their way to hardening back up. I let my guard down and for what? "I never beg. And here I started to allow my walls to come tumbling down for you. And the first chance you get, you turn me down."

His hands that were propped up on the mattress clenched as his jaw hardened. "I'm fucking this up." He let one of his hands drift to mine where they were firmly grasping the sheet and he pried it from my clutch. "I wasn't refusing you. God, I could never refuse you anything. I have to go into town before it starts getting dark to get things from the store for Bea and her husband and make sure Stella and Norah are all right." His thumb began rubbing in tiny circles on the hand he held, "I was trying to decide whether or not we had enough time before I have to go."

Well, that was one way of making me feel like a world class bitch. Dean was a nice guy, what on earth did he see in me? But then I remembered that this was only a fling. Two willing and able adults enjoying each other before the possibility of never seeing each other again arose. I didn't know what hurt worse, the fact that after this week Dean Parker would almost cease to exist for me, or the fact that I wanted to long for something more.

"I want to come," I said, not even thinking of letting him go out in these conditions by himself. I didn't know what help I could offer, but it would make me feel better if he wasn't braving it alone.

An even louder groan escaped from his lips, "Sweetheart, I have to get going. I am *definitely* calling a rain check though."

A slight giggle bubbled through me at the double entendre before I quickly sobered. I pushed his shoulder back as I swept my legs over the side of the bed and stood up. "Seriously?" I deadpanned, "that's not what I meant and you know it."

I padded around the room, still completely in the buff, retrieving my discarded clothes so I could get ready to leave with him. I felt his eyes on my backside as I pulled my panties and then my leggings up my thighs and it almost made me feel giddy. What the hell was wrong with me?

"What are you doing to me? Here I am, willingly going out with you just so I don't have to wonder whether or not you've gotten stuck under a monstrous snowdrift." I paused just a beat before continuing on, "I guess it's really more for my amusement." I was trying to cover up the deeper feelings that threatened to break free. I sat down on the edge of the bed, my back still to him, and slipped my arms into the straps of my satin bra and fastened the hooks at my back. Dean appeared in front of me, grabbed ahold of my upper arms and hauled me up and into his chest. My breath left me in a whoosh as our bodies aligned flush against one another.

I audibly swallowed and debated looking into his eyes, not knowing what I would find staring back at me? He took the decision away from me as he pressed his fingertips under my chin and tilted my face up so I had no other choice but to give him my attention.

His expression was smoldering and it became unbearably hard to breathe. When he spoke, his tone was laced with uncertain emotion. "I could ask you the same thing, what're you doing to me? But I don't want to spend the remainder of our time together trying to separate out our emotions. You said you wanted a fling and I'm seriously trying to keep up that mindset." A hint of sadness flashed behind his eyes before he released me and his expression turned impassive.

"Be ready to go in five minutes. I'm going to go warm up the truck."

As he walked out of the guest room, I couldn't help the niggling suspicion that I truly hurt his feelings when I only offered him a fling. I thought one measly romp between the sheets would be enough to get our fill of one another, but it seemed I was only lying to myself.

Stepping out into the garage, I pulled the door closed behind me and found Dean waiting in the driver's seat of Baylor's work truck. When he didn't make a move to look up through the windshield or even hop out to greet me, I knew that whatever this was between us was only hurting him. I didn't like the shift in our relationship and certainly didn't want to have to walk on eggshells around him. I swallowed past the lump in my throat, because I honestly didn't know how to proceed from here. Readjusting my wool knit hat on my head, ensuring it was covering my ears, I walked towards the passenger side. After Dean had walked out I'd rushed to Eden's bedroom and pilfered through her closet until I found her old purple parka and a pair of snow boots. Eden's foot was a size bigger than mine, but it'd work for the situation.

When I lifted the handle on the door I didn't know what the mood in the cab of the truck would be. What I didn't expect was the tension to be so unsurmountable that it would really take some effort to climb up into the seat.

I stayed frozen in my seat, looking out the windshield in disbelief at all the slide offs on the road. Numerous cars were driven into embankments and even more were abandoned. Dean hadn't even spoken a word to me since I situated myself and buckled up. He was driving carefully and I couldn't help but think maybe he was taking extra precautions because I was with him. Just the thought that he actually might care about me sent up all kinds of red flags that I wanted nothing more than to ignore. He was nothing like my two ex-husbands, so keeping him from my overly guarded heart wasn't fair to him or myself. I just didn't know whether or not it was worth the chance to break down my heavily defended wall only to have him shatter my heart even more. Then there was the matter of us living in two completely different states. I released a long, drawn out sigh and laid the back of my head up against the head rest. Twenty-four hours ago I barely tolerated the guy and now what?

"You like me..." Dean spoke up, startling me from my thoughts as if he had read my mind.

Placing my elbow on the door frame, I sighed again, thinking of how I should put my emotions into words. If I even wanted to give him that much. "I'm a step up from tolerating you, I'd say I'm accepting you. Ask me again tomorrow."

He chuckled, "I'll hold you to that." And just like that the tension dissipated; I was extremely thankful for the relief and the ability to take a fully cleansing breath.

Dean was right, I didn't want to spend the remainder of our time contemplating what the next step would be or obsess about something coming afterwards. I wanted to just *be* with him. "Can we just be Dean and Julia? No expectations or labels for the remainder of my trip?" I bit my lip and glanced in his direction, not knowing how he would take my request.

The tip of his mouth curled up into a small grin, "Yeah, we can do that."

Just as quickly as he grinned, his mouth turned into a grim line as he started veering to the side of the faint snow plowed road. I looked through the windshield as he pulled behind a small four door sedan which had the outline of people sitting in the front seats. He threw the truck in park, placed his hand on the door handle before pausing and looking back towards me, "Lock the door when I get out and keep your phone handy."

Anxiety flared in my stomach as I reached across the center console and grabbed ahold of his forearm. "What're you doing? You can't go out there." My feeling of panic had my voice trembling as I looked out through the windshield at the stalled vehicle in front of us.

"Julia, this isn't New York or Nashville," his eyes softened when he looked at my hand grasping him. "I'm just going to see if they need any help."

With that he opened the door, angling himself so he could jump out and onto the snow covered road. I never took my eyes off him for a second and even willed myself not to blink so I wouldn't miss anything. He leaned into the car when the owner rolled down the driver's side window. My hands gripped the plastic console and the door tightly as I quietly prayed that we wouldn't end up on the evening news or worse, America's Most Wanted as the victims of a ruthless murder when all the man wanted to do was help.

Dean looked relaxed which caused me to ease some of my anxiety. He even threw his head back to laugh a time or two. That man had such a beautiful heart to help out a family who was stuck. I watched as he shoved himself off the car and walked towards the bumper. I was now almost flush with the dashboard just trying to get a better view of what was going down. He flashed me a gorgeous smile that made my stomach flip. He braced both hands on the trunk of the car and started to push while the toes of his boots dug into the snow below him.

He almost made the whole process look easy but I'm sure he was exerting himself, being that he was trying to get the car unstuck by himself. I saw the tires move back and forth a few times and within a few short minutes the car was free. A hand stuck out from the driver's side window to bid farewell as they slowly took off down the road towards their destination.

Dean shoved his hands into his pockets and smiled lightly to himself as he came rounding the side of the truck. Once he lifted himself into the cab he placed his gloved hands in front of the heat vent to warm them up a touch. I didn't know whether to commend him for his bravery or chastise his ass for his blatant stupidity.

Chapter 14

Dean

My hands were numb from having to push the ice cold car; I needed to remember to pick up some weather-resistant gloves. When I was approaching the stalled car I tried to talk myself out of it several times. Not only was I placing myself in immediate danger, but Julia as well. I would never blatantly place Julia in any danger. And while the crime rate was scarce in Cottage Grove, it wasn't entirely out of the question for something to happen.

Turns out it was Mr. Samson, a sixty-something-year-old man with dark skin, and his wife Edna. They were on their way home after risking the road conditions when they started veering off the road and ultimately got stuck. I offered to call them a tow truck but he insisted they could make it home if only he could get moving again. Several cars had passed theirs, but I was the only one to stop, so I knew that I had made the right decision in checking things out a little closer. I would just accept the consequences of my actions when I got back into the truck with Julia.

My body shivered as I was trying to warm up a bit before taking off the direction of Eden's father's grocery store. I looked at Julia who had her mouth gaping open but an indifferent expression on her face. I quirked a brow, getting ready to find out exactly what was running through her head when she launched her upper body across the console and sealed her lips with mine. The kiss completely came from left field but it was frantic and was warming me right up from the inside. She was conveying through her kiss just how scared she was but glad that I had made it back in one piece.

All too quickly she pulled away from me and righted herself in her seat, but not before sucker punching me in the arm.

"Ow!" I hollered a bit too loud in the small confines of the truck. I rubbed my hand along my throbbing skin. "What the hell was that for?"

"For being a stupid jerk! I had to kiss you because you were back and that was such a noble and friendly thing you did. But at the same time I had to sock you because it was utterly reckless and moronic! Do you not watch the news or read the newspapers? That type of thing," she flicked her wrist towards where the stalled car had been, "could've gotten you killed!"

She huffed out a breath before buckling herself and crossing her arms in front of her chest. Her lips were red from where she'd forcefully kissed me and her remaining anger was radiating from her pores. She was cute as hell.

I placed the truck in drive and carefully pulled back out onto the main road, continuing on with our little adventure. The more I thought about the whole situation, I tended to agree with her that it was incredibly stupid but there wasn't much I could do about it now. It was engrained into my soul to help people whenever I could, so that's what I did without thinking about the consequences beforehand. *Typical male* my mother would regale.

I couldn't help the bright smile that formed on my face and the amusing chuckle that bubbled up from my chest. "What's so damn funny?" Julia questioned, her anger still very much in place.

Her hostility only made me laugh harder. I loved the fact that I could get such a rise out of her. "You kissing me and then punching me for what I'd done, yeah, you like me..." I wasn't giving her any room to argue, so I pressed a button on the dash to turn the radio on and turned the knob up to put a cease to any further talking. She would only be lying to herself, so I was making things easier on her.

A little more than a half an hour later, we were finally pulling into the parking lot of Mr. Richardt's grocery store. Normally, it'd only take us ten minutes or so but with the road conditions and the fact that I thought it was hilarious that Julia was still pouting in the corner, I decided to make sure I took my time.

Earlier when we had left Baylor and Eden's house I didn't want to come across as broody, but I knew that if I spoke to her I'd end up saying something that I would regret. Like pleading with her to consider staying or rather telling her that we shouldn't see each other for the rest of the time she was here. There was no doubt that spending this much time with her would make things infinitely worse on me when the time came for her to leave. But I would risk my heart to be near her as much as she would allow. I meant what I said, that I would try and keep the mindset that this was all a fling, but I didn't think I could convince my heart of the same thing. It already knew what it wanted and it wanted without a shadow of a doubt to claim Julia Caldwell.

I jumped from the cab and shut my door before hurrying around to Julia's to help her out. I offered her my hand which she stared at before reluctantly taking in her embrace. She kept her hand in mine as we crossed the snow-plowed parking lot and only released it when she went to retrieve a shopping cart. I pulled my list from the inside pocket of my coat and we set off gathering the things that were needed by Stella and Bea. Walking side by side, it seemed almost domesticated. I wanted to imagine the possibility of Julia and I doing this weekly, but pushed it further back in my mind.

"Why are we getting things for Stella? Why not Bentley, he is her son."

Because Bentley most likely couldn't be bothered, is what I wanted to come out saying, that he was probably still in bed with his hussy of the week. "We were already heading out so I told Stella that it wasn't an inconvenience. Besides, Norah is with her, so it gives me the opportunity to check in on her." Not a complete lie, but not the entire truth either.

"You really love Norah, huh?" Her tone became soft as if she was trying to understand.

"More than anything and as if she were my own." Sofie, my first wife, couldn't understand why I had to fly out of Texas back to Oregon for the birth of my God-daughter. That should've been my number one clue that things weren't going to work out between the two of us, my family always came first and she didn't feel that way. But once those little blue eyes landed on mine, I was a goner. There was nothing I wouldn't do for that little girl.

We resumed walking up and down each aisle, getting little things for us to snack on throughout the week as well. "Dean, can I ask you a question?" She stopped walking and looked up to me.

"You just did."

Rolling her eyes she continued, "Do you want kids of your own someday?"

I wasn't expecting such a personal question to come from her, but I didn't even need to take a moment to think. "Absolutely." Thinking back to Kate, I could've had a child with her.

"Why do you look so sad?"

"Oh, I was just thinking about my second wife, Kate. We tried for a long time to have kids, even going to different fertility specialists. The day I thought she was going to surprise me and say we were going to be parents was the day that I found her in bed with a random guy that she'd met at the supermarket one day and they'd hit it off. It was ironically the same day that she informed me that she was having his baby."

Her hand flew to her mouth as she gasped in astonishment. I didn't want her to pity me, but what was reflected in her eyes was nothing more than pure empathy. "My second husband cheated on me as well. He was only interested in himself and that damn dog of his. Like I've said before, the only thing he ever gave me was my boobs and that was purely for his benefit. He said they weren't adequate enough for him. I was blinded by love and let him berate me as he saw fit."

I couldn't help but to see red as anger flashed in my eyes. Her husband talked down to her and emotionally abused her? No wonder she was guarded like Fort Knox and reserved about getting closer to men in any way other than a purely physical sense.

She shrugged her shoulder, "It's all right, it's all in the past now. Besides, Paul was harmless in the physical sense. And at that particular time in my life it was what I needed."

"What you should always need is to feel safe and protected in any relationship and any guy who doesn't provide that for you isn't a man at all." I placed a hand on her hip and whispered close to her ear, "But you should also always feel desirable and wanted. He was a fucking idiot to not see the special beauty who was right in front of him." She turned her head away from me as if she couldn't fathom that a man would actually be nice to her and want to spend his time with her.

The way she worded her earlier statement made me question something that crossed my mind. "What about your first husband?" Her head whipped around until her eyes connected with mine and fear immediately set in on her face. She was truly terrified.

"Logan? I don't *ever* talk about him, I don't even want to give him the satisfaction of *thinking* of him. Story time is officially over." She began walking away from me, her hands clenching the handle of the cart. I hurried after her, quickly catching up before she turned the corner. In the next aisle she finally looked up from her purse and spotted Mr. Richardt, Eden's father, and I could see her face light up.

With what she had just revealed to me, the pieces were starting to form together about Julia's first husband, Logan. She never indulged in anything other than inconspicuous details, but it was blaringly obvious that Logan was a downright bastard and not only hurt Julia emotionally, but physically as well. The reason why Julia acted the way that she did, putting on a front for everyone, was becoming abundantly clear. I just had to show her that not all men were like her ex-husbands. That I wasn't one of them.

"Mr. Richardt, it's so good to see you!" Julia exclaimed, before pulling him into her arms for a brief embrace. She acted as if she hadn't seen the man in months rather than just yesterday at Eden's wedding. Once they released each other, he took a second to look from her to me and back again.

"Is he being nice to you, Jules?" Richard indicated towards me with a jerk of his chin. "Eden told me that you two hadn't been getting along, then I find you in here together." He eyed me warily before kneeling back down in front of the box of produce he was restocking. He pulled out a crate of bananas and stood with a stagger before placing them in front of the display to make things easier for himself.

"Oh he's being just fine, Rich, nothing to worry about."

Why in the world were they making me sound like I was a predator or something? Or that it wasn't all Julia's fault that we bickered worse than an old married couple?

"Well, that's where you're wrong, you're one of my girls and I always worry about my girls. Eden not as much since she's in the same town as me now and only a phone call away. And even if they are hanging out with Dean here, who I've known since he was knee high to a grasshopper."

Julia sniffled and quickly wiped clean the evidence of the tear rolling down her cheek.

"I'm good, Mr. Richardt, I promise." She walked back into his outstretched arms, and then whispered in his ear which had his gaze finding mine. Again, what the hell? "We must be going, we have things to drop off before we head back home."

She let the word home roll off her tongue with such ease that I was sure she hadn't even realized what she'd said. Oh, we were going home all right. To *my* home.

By the time we pulled into Baylor and Eden's driveway, it was well past dark. I killed the engine and just waited to see how Julia was doing. It had been an emotional day, with a lot to take in for the both of us, but it really opened my eyes to how Julia could really be.

Besides the Richardts and the Jenkinses, Julia really didn't have any family that cared for her. And despite everything she had told me she'd been through and the blanks I'd filled in myself, she truly had a beautiful soul when she put her reservations aside and opened her heart and her mind.

She made it through the Norah inquisition as to why we had arrived together with perfect poise. And listening to a twelve-year-old without sending any sarcastic barbs her way was an accomplishment for Julia. She knew just how important and special my Norah Bean was to me, and it awoke another part of me when I saw that she was making a conscientious effort to heed her tongue.

Then we went to Bea and Earl's. Beatrice fussed over Julia as if she was her own daughter, if they had ever been blessed with children. Bea was like another mother to me, but also acted as my secretary as well. We got along so well that I thought nothing of the fact that she pulled me aside and harped on me for not telling her of the raving beauty in the other room. How was I supposed to tell anyone anything when there really wasn't much to tell?

The last stop on my list was my parents' house, although I *may* have left out that tiny detail to Julia. She *may* have given me the stink eye, which *may* have held promise of retaliation of the castration variety that would occur later. After a few awkward moments and some even more awkward introductions, she warmed right up to my momma. And my mother took an instant liking to her, too. After she gushed about how beautiful Julia was, she insisted that we stay for dinner. Stealing glances at one another and idle touches was all that had passed between the two of us since her stolen kiss in the truck earlier and I was more than ready to feel her body against mine again.

"I don't know about you, but I'm tired," she said as she lifted her arms as high as the inside of the truck would allow, trying to stretch. "This has been a long day. I plan on sleeping until noon tomorrow and then lounging around on the couch the rest of the day." I wondered if this was her not-so-subtle way of trying to get rid of me, but she wasn't doing the best job of it. I wasn't going to go down without a fight. And if there was one thing to say about me, I didn't always play fair.

"Did you ever have any holiday traditions growing up with your nanny?" I was resorting to useless chitchat, but I didn't want to lose her company, not yet.

She briefly lifted a brow before she looked down at her hands which were linked together, resting in her lap. "Nanny always bought me an ornament every year. Didn't matter what kind of ornament it was, I have all different ones ranging from poseable nutcrackers to a pink French poodle." She chuckled mildly. "But they all had to have the year engraved on them, it was her thing." Her voice grew sad as she released a sigh, and lifted her head, "I still have every single one she ever gave me, up until 2010, when she passed."

I reached over the console and picked up the hand closest to me, brought it towards my mouth, and turned it over so I could place a single kiss in the center of her palm. Then I took in her wide-eyed expression, which was an improvement from being sad just seconds before. "Thank you for today. I haven't had this much fun in a long time." I knew how to lay it on thick, but this was different because it was entirely true. Even when we were peeved at one another it was still enjoyable. Never a dull moment between the two of us.

I wasn't sure if I had rendered her speechless or if she was having a hard time speaking past her emotions, so she nodded her head.

"Why don't you go pack a small bag and meet me back at my place? We can watch a movie while we relax on the couch together."

She lifted a brow and questioned, "Why?"

"Because that's where I live. And if you recall, I have a little matter of a rain check from this morning that I intend to use and I'd rather hear you scream my name in *my* bed in *my* house."

Her cheeks turned the faintest of pinks and it was always glorious to see her blush. She said nothing more before hopping out of the truck and letting herself inside Baylor and Eden's house. I guess we'd see if she'd show.

Twenty minutes later, I had a fire started in my living room fireplace and had changed into a long-sleeved black Henley tee and flannel pajama bottoms. There were a few Christmas movies saved to my DVR; all that was missing was Julia. I was about to give up on her coming over, when I heard a soft knock at the door.

Whenever I saw Julia, even put together with her impeccable outfits and her flawless hair and makeup, I was never prepared. But when she waltzed in with her hair thrown up in a bun on top of her head and her face void of any makeup, much as she had looked in the morning, I was struck dumb and rendered speechless. She was a vision, plain and simple. Someone up above was rewarding me and I wouldn't take it for granted.

She unzipped her coat and slid it down her arms which pushed out her chest towards me and good God almighty, she was braless. I had to put my fist in my mouth and bite down on a finger so I could calm myself down a bit before I threw her over my shoulder and hauled her ass to my bed.

Suddenly, I felt shy and didn't know what to say or do next. "I thought we'd watch a Christmas movie, is that ok with you?"

Her eyes lit up, "Can I pick?"

"As long as it's not Elf or A Christmas Story, I'm sure Norah will have us watching them on a continuous loop closer to the day."

"Christmas Vacation!" She exclaimed and then rushed to take a seat on the edge of the couch as if she would burst if we couldn't watch it right away. Wasn't she supposedly tired?

I turned on the movie and then purposely sat right beside her, not giving any amount of wiggle room even though I had the rest of the sectional at my disposal.

"Seriously?" She looked down at our legs which were practically touching and then to me. "Haven't you ever heard of personal space?"

"That must've been one of those manners my mom didn't instill in me," I muttered, feigning a mock apology.

"Oh bull, I've met your momma, you can't use her as an excuse for your own lack of manners." She shoved my arm before popping up off of the couch and going around my giant ottoman towards the other side of the couch. I knew she wasn't expecting me to come after her because once my arms wound around her waist, she released a loud squeal. She tried to pry my arms away while she kicked her legs frantically. I flopped her down on her back and covered her body with my own. To add to her amusement, I skimmed my hands down her sides until I reached just above her hip bone. And I brought on a fully torturous tickle assault. She had tears streaming down her face and her chest was heaving as she tried to take in big gulps of air. "Stop, Dean!" She yelled. "I'm gonna pee!!" She yelled next and I automatically stopped moving my hands. When a woman yelled those three words, it was the universal signal for STOP, cease all movement.

I allowed her to take a few deep breaths of air; my body was aligned perfectly in between her legs and with the close proximity that we were to one another she was bound to know that I was turned on. Once her breathing had almost returned to normal, I removed my hands from her waist only to bring them directly up underneath her arms. Each hand moved in symmetrical fashion as she fleetingly lost control over her body once again. "Dean! Please stop," she said between fits of laughter. The sound of her infectious giggling traveled down my spine and in no time I was laughing right along with her. She was instinctively wriggling her body, trying to move away from my grasp. And as her body was fighting underneath mine she would brush up against my erection, only making me want to take her more.

Her loose pajama pants would be so easy to slip down her legs. God, I needed her naked.

She strenuously lifted her head up off of the couch cushion and started bringing her mouth towards my face. My first instinct was that she was attempting to bite me in order for me to stop what I was doing. I flinched back but not before her tongue darted out from her mouth and licked a line along my cheek. The wetness warmed my skin. If she really wanted to play games I could show her something for her to lick.

I halted my hands in place and peered into her eyes while raising a brow, "Did you just lick me, really?" She pursed her lips together as if she was almost daring me to do something about it. "So what does this mean, since you licked me I'm yours or something?"

She made no attempts to cover up her amusement, barking out a laugh directly in my face. "You'd like that, wouldn't you?"

Dean and Julia bantering once again. Don't tell anyone, but my heart actually swelled.

I leaned on my forearm, still suspended above her, and took my free hand to grip my chest, "Absolutely, consider it one of my items on my bucket list. Can we mark it off yet?" I knew that I was treading on rough waters and at any moment she could tip my boat completely over. Was I a strong enough swimmer to endure the current?

Expecting a sarcastic rebuttal, the only thing I saw was wanting, deep in her eyes as she stared at my lips. I leaned forward, not wanting to break the moment, and fused my lips together with hers. This time things weren't going to be rushed or frantic. She was in my house so it was my chance to savor her completely. Show her exactly how a woman should be relished.

Chapter 15

Julia

Dean was moving almost in slow motion. I could tell he wanted to take his time and live for the moment. But going slow didn't work for me, it reminded me of making love and that's not what we were doing. We were fucking, plain and simple. No, going slow would add the elusive grey area into the mix and I didn't need that when my feelings had already begun to fall off-kilter and I was leaving in only a few short days. This was supposed to be nothing more than a fling, dammit. I had to think of something.

He brought his leg up under my covered knee and moved it towards my stomach. I felt his warm hand encircle my bare ankle up under my pajama pants. My breath hitched in my throat as he continued to run his hand up my calf, ascending towards my knee. After he finally released my mouth, he began trailing open-mouthed kisses down my neck all the way to my collarbone, stopping only because of the barrier of my flimsy t-shirt.

Whatever I was thinking before about needing to go fast flew out the window when he sat back on his haunches and lifted his own shirt over his head, throwing it to the ground. The heat that coursed through me at the sight of his bare, sculpted chest was enough to render me completely useless. He brought his hands up under my arms to help me into a sitting position before he fiddled with the bottom edges to my shirt. In one fell swoop my arms were above my head and my shirt had joined his along the floor. My nipples pebbled at attention once they were met with the cool air. Goose bumps broke out along my naked torso at the anticipation of what was to come. And hopefully this time it would be me.

130

I wondered why things between us fell into place so easily and felt so right. I was waiting for the anxiety to present itself at the mere thought of giving whatever this was between us a chance. Maybe it was hiding, buried deep in the recesses of my soul, and would make itself known at the most inopportune time.

Dean raised up from his position on the couch and picked up my hand that was resting on my pajama-clad knee. I briefly thought he was going to end up moving this party to his bedroom, but when he pushed me back onto his overstuffed ottoman I wasn't sure of anything anymore.

He hooked his fingers under my pajama pants and quickly dragged them down my legs until they too, were hanging out with the pile of clothes among the floor. Dean went down to his knees in front of me, his hands clasping both of my knees before prying them apart. When I felt the startling sensation of his tongue licking over the bare flesh of my inner thigh all the way to my weeping core, I released a breathy moan.

I looked up to find his eyes locked on mine as he ascended up my body and pressed a kiss on my pubic bone, directly above where I needed him the most. I could push his head down in between my legs and silently demand he did his diligence, but this was Dean we were talking about. He got off on making me struggle for things, in no way would he make this easy.

"Dean, baby, I need more!" I could see a thrill shivering through him and I knew it was because I called him baby. I didn't have time to dwell on the nickname because in that same exact second he plundered his head between my legs grabbed ahold of my clit between his teeth and sucked, hard. I was already so completely riled up that I knew it wouldn't take me long to find my release. I felt as his fingertips traveled up began circling around the very edge of my core before diving into my wet heat.

I was panting, growing closer and closer to orgasm when Dean took his mouth and fingers completely away. I wanted to protest, I wanted to scream and kick with an unabashed tantrum. But he quickly pushed his pants down his legs, lined up his throbbing erection and slammed it home.

My legs encircled his waist of their own accord as I placed my hands along his cheeks so I could pull him in for a kiss. "Fuck me, Dean! I need you to fuck me hard!" My kiss was frantic and demanding, spilling all of my feelings of want in that one lone kiss.

His mouth worked against mine, swallowing all of my cries as he continued to thrust himself inside of me. "Perfect, Julia. So fucking perfect," his voice was rough against my lips as the onslaught of my orgasm began to build again. My thighs tightened around his hips as the rush of pleasure exploded and my orgasm took over. My hips bucked, trying to get closer to him as his hands reached underneath me to grab the flesh of my ass. I felt a hard bite at my shoulder as he sunk his teeth into me and pumped into me furiously once, twice, three more times until his own release spiraled through him. He slumped forward, each of us trying to get a handle on our wild and labored breathing. Sex had never been like this, I was afraid that I was already addicted to Dean's touch. No one in Nashville would be able to compare to the explosive chemistry that we shared in and out of the bedroom. I didn't want to think about the future because that's not what I needed. This was supposed to be a one-time fling and nothing more, could I even allow myself to hope of something more to come from this?

I never got the chance to answer that question, not even wanting that statement to cross my mind. Everything was ruined and I knew that I couldn't trust myself around him.

Dean slowly began to pull out and I felt a major wetness seep out while he was doing so. I knew what had happened before he even said a word. Bile rose to the back of my throat at the risk we just took. How could I be so stupid?

"Fuck! I didn't use a condom."

It was Wednesday morning. Three days before I was originally supposed to leave and a full day since I'd talked to Dean, not for his lack of trying. I rolled my suitcase through the kitchen and laundry room of Eden's house and left it sitting right next to the garage door. I was extremely thankful that most of the snow had melted and I was able to switch my return ticket to an earlier flight. It took heavy coercion and two hundred additional dollars just to do so, but I would've paid two thousand, just to get away from Dean Parker.

Sure, it was a dual effort in forgetting the condom but I felt as if I just couldn't be around him any longer. In no time my barriers came tumbling down around him and I let details get thrown by the wayside. Such impactful details that could've led to a tiny human growing inside me right that second. I wasn't cut out to be a mother, the thought alone terrified me and rattled me to my core. He had apologized so profusely that I almost wanted to cave and have mercy on him, but then I'd be back at square one once again.

The horn honking out in the driveway caused me to hurry up making sure the house was completely secured. I quickly ran through the house making sure all the lights were turned off and checked the lock on the front door before rushing through the laundry room. Grabbing the handle on my rolling suitcase, I pulled it through the door to the garage before turning around and making sure that door was locked and secured as well. As I walked out through the garage I wasn't expecting to see Dean leaning against the driver's side door to the cab. His face was hard as stone and his movements were terse as he spoke to the cab driver.

I had almost reached the front of the yellow vehicle, when he promptly put the car in reverse and backed out of the driveway before quickly speeding off. I dropped the handle to my suitcase and threw both of my arms in the air. "What the hell, Dean? That was my ride to the airport!"

He spread his legs out so his stance was wide and crossed his arms over his chest and narrowed his eyes to me. "I'm taking you to the airport." I opened my mouth to protest, "I'm not fucking playing, Julia. If you want to leave early to get away from me, fine. But I'm going to be the one to drive you to ease my mind a bit that you make it there." His tone was hard and didn't leave any room for bullshit. The hussy that I was had to squeeze my legs together by his take-charge attitude.

I said nothing as I grabbed the handle to my suitcase again and began walking towards Dean's garage. He released a long, drawn-out sigh and looked up to the clear sky, most likely asking for patience. I didn't ask him to scare off my ride and take me himself; actually I preferred it if he didn't. I hadn't even told him that I was leaving for this very reason, I wasn't good at goodbyes. I was trying to make things easier on the both of us.

It was time to steel myself in armor and pretend I wasn't in the present with this gaping hollow feeling in the center cavity of my chest. This is why I didn't deal with gushy feelings, I'd rather not feel like this, I'd rather be numb and not feel at all.

Chapter 16

Dean

The damn woman was so infuriating. She wasn't even going to tell me goodbye. I heard a horn coming from next door, so I rushed to grab my coat and ran outside. When I saw the yellow cab sitting in Baylor's driveway, my heart sank. She wasn't supposed to leave for three more days. We hadn't even sat down and worked anything out. My feet carried me over to the driver's side where the middle-aged bald man took his leisurely time, turning the crank to partially roll down his window.

"Yeah?" He barked through the crack.

"Where is the fare headed?" I checked in the garage to make sure she hadn't come out yet.

"It's none of your business," he immediately snapped back. He mustn't be aware that he was messing with a severely pissed-off man who would stop at nothing to get the woman.

My patience was almost nonexistent and I thought he could tell by my tightened jaw and clenched fists that were resting against the paned glass.

"She's headed to the airport," he finally spoke as he faced forward.

I slipped my hand into my back pocket and pulled out my wallet. I grabbed a fifty dollar bill as I heard the door inside the garage slam. I folded the bill in half and shoved it in between the parted glass before pushing myself away from the car. "Hurry up and get the hell out of here."

More Than A Fling

Which brought us to now, me white knuckling the steering wheel in my car. Seemed to be a common theme with Julia. Just a little over a week ago we were in an extremely similar but different situation, but no less tense. Her shoulders were stiff and her back ramrod straight. She was completely on edge and wouldn't let her defenses down for a second. She looked to be ready for a fight at a moment's notice. Any form of communication would be better than what was taking place right now.

My heart panged in my chest and I longed to take her hand in mine. I didn't know if she was scared of the possibility of being pregnant. She needed to know that I regretted nothing and if she was indeed carrying my child I would embrace her and the baby into my life with open arms. This could really be a blessing in disguise.

I loosened up my hold on the steering wheel and spoke just above a whisper. "Would it be so bad?"

She looked at me with her mouth gaping open as if she was flabbergasted I would've asked such a question. "Would it be so bad if I was pregnant? Yes, Dean, yes it would be awful."

My stomach sank. At least I had her answer even though it wasn't one that I was particularly expecting. No further elaboration from her as to why it would be so awful though. "Why? Why would it be such a terrible thing, Julia? Why can't you open up to me, don't you hate keeping people out?" My voice had risen now to where I was almost yelling.

She slammed her fist down on the dashboard, the sound resonating throughout the small space of the car and screamed at me. She took all of her pent up frustration and rolled it into one outburst and let it all out. "You want to know why I keep most people out and why Eden is the only one who knows me the most? Hell, she doesn't even know this part. My first husband abused me, he took all his frustration and anger out on me and beat me numerous times within an inch of my life!" Hearing what I had obviously suspected did nothing to squash down my temper; if anything it made me want to lash out at the man who had attempted to break Julia. "He pursued me because he knew I had money, although as I've told you,

136

I've never touched my trust fund until last week. And he didn't like that. So I was his own personal punching bag. I used to be sweet and naïve and was fucking stupid because I stayed with him because I thought I loved him and I was afraid that if I left he would stop at nothing to hunt me down and kill me. It took my nanny coming to visit me and seeing the evidence of his beatings for me to get away from him. I took the stand at his trial and my heart literally crumbled in my chest leaving an empty cavity." Tears were mercilessly streaming down her face and she took a moment to take a deep breath before she continued on. I couldn't believe what I was hearing, that my strong Julia had been through so much. "I fought to become this person, this shell of what I used to be. It's all I know now. Then I met Paul and knew since he had money he would want nothing to do with mine. He didn't physically hurt me, but I emotionally took a beat-down. He was jealous, and in so many words jealousy is manipulation. And that was his major goal, to manipulate me. Once he was out of my life I vowed that I wouldn't ever let another man hurt me. So I stuck to flings, one night stands, relationships that couldn't get messy. Then I met this wonderful guy, he didn't take any of my bullshit and I finally thought that I could be myself around him. So, naturally I let my walls come crumbling down. Things got hot and heavy and I loved every second of it, but I got careless." The fact wasn't lost on me that she was discussing us. She wiped another tear off of her face. We had arrived at the airport and I had parked rear the front entrance. I went to reach for her and she moved herself out of my reach.

"And he wants to know why it would be the end of the world if I was pregnant with his baby. I'm not mother material. After what I've been through in my lifetime I never wanted to bring a child into the mix. The fact that when I felt your reaction I felt dread all the way down to my bones and bile in my throat at the thought of me having a baby proves that. I can't do this, Dean." She looked so weak, nothing like the strong woman I knew she could be. She was breaking my heart. Breaking it apart into little pieces by her own hands. "I'm a coward, I wasn't even going to say goodbye to you, I was going to run away like the shameful bitch that I am." She placed her hand on the handle to open the door. This was it, she was leaving me. My feelings didn't matter at all. "Take a bow, Dean, you made the cold bitch believe in love again. And look where it got us." She turned her body away from me, ready to tuck her tail between her legs and run.

"Stay," it was the only word I could get to form around the lump in my throat. Tears were glistening in my eyes, threatening to topple over. She turned towards me and pulled her bottom lip in between her teeth and seemed to mull over the decision as to whether she could do just that. The fact that she was taking the time to think it over made hope bloom in my heart.

She took her eyes off of mine, and angled her body back towards the door. "I can't."

And with those two words I knew this was it, this was our finality. What had just bloomed into hope and seemed attainable quickly deflated resulting in utter despair. I was numb and I owed it all to Julia Caldwell. My third chance at love and my second chance at having a family, slipping through my fingers once again. This time it hurt infinitely worse, even though it had been mere days.

She surprised me by quickly leaning across the console and pressing her closed lips to my cheek. "Goodbye, Dean." And with that she grabbed her suitcase from the backseat before slamming the door and walking out of my life. Then and only then did I allow the tears to spill over the edge.

Numb. That's how I wanted to stay. I didn't want to feel this brick sitting in the middle of my chest any longer. It was the Monday after Julia's abrupt departure and the pain hadn't lessened a bit; if anything it had intensified tenfold. What made matters worse was that Baylor and Eden had gotten back into town from their honeymoon and I'd avoided them at all costs. What little was left of my heart wouldn't be able to take their happiness and being all lovey dovey around each other. I was well aware that made me a shitty friend, but I just needed some time.

Throwing the wooden door to Tillie's Tavern open, I stalked inside, immediately loosening my tie from around my neck. I'd been in such a horrible mood that Bea even yelled at me and she had never raised her voice at me before. She took it upon herself to cancel my last appointment for the day and sent me home as if she was my boss. I was internally grateful.

I slid into an empty stool at the bar and signaled the bartender with a lift of my finger.

He acknowledged me with a lift of his chin and then stopped in front of me, throwing his towel over his shoulder. "What'll it be?" I had no idea who the guy was, but at the moment I was glad it was anyone but Maisie. I didn't need to add her bullshit on top of everything else.

"I'll have a scotch." I needed something strong that would go down easy. After a few of those I wouldn't be feeling much of anything.

"Coming right up." He set off towards the other end of the bar to retrieve a fresh, clean glass and a hand interrupted my thoughts as it skimmed across my back.

I turned to my left and couldn't stop the frown from forming on my lips at the sight of Maisie. Shit, I thought I had dodged that bullet.

"Hiya, babe," she purred, as she tried to snake her hand across my chest before I circled my hand around her forearm and gave her a less than gentle squeeze to inform her that I wasn't interested.

"Dammit, Maisie, quit trying to be so fucking desperate, it's not attractive. At first I thought the whole act was endearing, but now I see you for what you really are...pathetic." Tears immediately welled up in her eyes as she brought her hands to her face and ran off towards the back. The bartender sat down my scotch and I snatched it from the counter before throwing it straight down my throat, the trail igniting as it made its way to my stomach. I slammed down the empty glass and lifted my head, "Keep 'em coming." I didn't mean to snap at Maisie, it wasn't fair for her to be the outlet of my anger. But the damn woman was ruthless and just couldn't take a fucking hint.

"What's with the foul mood?" Tillie showed up beside me at the bar, turning her stool so she was looking in my direction and propped an elbow on the wooden bar top.

"I'm sorry, Ms. Tillie. It was a momentary lapse in judgement, I had no right to lash out at her. I'll find Maisie and apologize to her later."

"Nonsense," she lifted a haggard finger in the air, signaling to the bartender to bring her a beer. "Maisie is a hard-headed woman. It was high time someone put her in her place—trying to pick up any and every guy that crosses the threshold into my bar. Hell, the only reason I keep her around is because I'm forced to. Don't get me wrong, I love my granddaughter, but she doesn't have too much going on upstairs, if you know what I mean," she joked as she pointed to her brain.

She looked past me briefly before bringing her eyes back to mine. "Where is your lady friend?" My face fell. "Oh," she exclaimed as she took a pull of the beer that had appeared in front of her. "That's what this pout fest is all about."

I sighed and took a sip from my fresh scotch, letting the glass dangle from my fingertips. "She's not my lady. Not my decision though." I looked at her with hurt in my eyes and shrugged a shoulder. "She didn't love me enough to stay."

"Bullshit," she said point blank. "No one spends five thousand dollars on a guy at an auction for shits and giggles."

"Even if she did, she doesn't have those feelings for me anymore."

"That's where you're wrong. Women, especially ones like that pistol Julia, don't just turn their feelings off and on like a leaky faucet. Boy, are you wanting to throw in the towel or throw down the gauntlet? You need to show some perseverance and not give up on her." She allowed her gaze to travel down my seated form and lingered a little longer than necessary at my crotch, making me raise a lip in distaste, as she muttered under her breath, "I'm sure you've got oodles of stamina too." I could see where Maisie got it from. She waved a hand, "Give her some time to gather her feelings without making her feel overwhelmed. Then try and talk to her. Did you let her know how you feel?"

I shook my head in response, "I tried, but she wouldn't let me."

"Make her listen to you. But like I said, give her a bit of time first." She waved her hands around in the air in front of her towards my body, "All of this can be a bit overwhelming."

With her strange version of advice she drained the remainder of her beer and slid off of the stool and disappeared into the back, leaving me to my own devices.

After I had successfully downed my third scotch, music began playing from behind me. Realizing what it was I released a groan out of pure annoyance. I couldn't believe that the fact that it was Monday, therefore karaoke night, didn't even cross my mind. If I had remembered, then I would've stayed clear of this place. As if I needed anything else that reminded me of Julia. Her scent lingering on my ottoman was more than enough.

I needed more to drink. I impatiently threw up my arm indicating my urgent need for a refill. The alcohol was doing its job, coursing through my veins on the way to helping lessen the pain in my heart. The sweltering heat in this place had forced me out of my suit jacket after scotch number two. And now here I was taking off my cufflinks and tossing them on the bar, watching them scatter along the surface and spin like tops, so I could roll up the sleeves on my pale green dress shirt.

My posture slumped forward on the bar stool as I placed my elbows on the counter. I'm sure I looked pathetic, but there wasn't anything I wanted more than to continue to drown my sorrows. Tomorrow...No, I'm sure I'd be nursing a tremendous hangover, but by Wednesday I'd be more than ready to do everything in my power to get Julia back. That should be more than enough time for her and since it would be Christmas Eve I would have a legitimate excuse to reach out to her. Fuck, I didn't know much about women when it came to things such as this. Would that even be enough time? Was it almost Christmas already? I hadn't even felt like putting up my tree and still didn't. The day could just roll right by this year for all I cared.

No, my mind was made up, she *would* be hearing from me on Wednesday.

The bartender sat my drink down on a new napkin this time and I clasped my hand around the sweaty condensation around the glass to drag it closer towards me. I was few sips in, enjoying the solitude I had created when a hand slapped me on my right shoulder. *So much for being alone*, I thought but quickly regretted it when Baylor appeared to my left.

He ordered himself a beer before he took a seat next to me. "Hey man, haven't seen you in a while."

"Yeah," I nodded, as I took another sip, feeling the cool liquid coat my throat. "I've been meaning to stop by since y'all got back, but I've been busy." I was astonished that the lie rolled off of my tongue so easily. Baylor was my oldest friend and any other time I'd be chomping at the bit to hear all about his and Eden's honeymoon. Well, maybe not *all* about it. There were some things I just didn't need to know about. I should be happy for the two of them and I was, but I just didn't want to dwell on it given how unhappy I was.

I mustered up all my strength and prepared to tune out all the mushy, sappy details, which I was sure would be the majority of the story. "So how was the honeymoon?"

Baylor lifted his bottle of beer to his lips and took a hefty swig before placing it on the smooth wooden surface. "It was good, fantastic actually." And that was all he said. Someone upstairs needed a high fucking five for taking mercy on me because Baylor didn't elaborate.

"I'll let Eden reminisce all the details for you, within reason," he grinned to himself and I found myself tipping up a corner of my mouth.

"Hey, uh, did you take Julia to the airport last week?"

My throat bobbed as I gulped and quickly brought my glass to my lips so I would have something to take my focus off of the pain of remembering what went down when I took her to the airport.

"Sure did," I replied evenly.

"Did she seem all right to you? Eden has called her a few times, but she said Julia just seems kind of off, maybe sad even. But won't say anything to her about it." My leg started involuntarily bouncing underneath the bar as a cold sweat broke out across my forehead. I tried playing things cool but the second I averted my eyes from his, he knew something was up.

His hand slammed down on the counter, rattling the liquid in my glass, "Dammit, Dean, what'd you do?"

I jerked my head in his direction and said a little louder that I intended to, "Me? Why would you automatically assume it was something I did?!"

"Well, did you?" He asked as he gave me a knowing glance and narrowing his eyes.

I quickly released my breath, deflating my lungs completely of air. I needed to take a second to rein in my anger, if not I'd be lashing out at Baylor because my defenses were up.

I paused briefly to carefully think of what I should and shouldn't disclose.

"What happened was that I went and fell in love with her and she pretty much wants nothing to do with me." It was weird finally hearing the words that had been swirling around in my head come out for the very first time. "In the short amount of time knowing Julia, I fell in love with her. She came roaring through like a cyclone destroying everything in her path, including my heart." I cringed at how pitiful I sounded. Being in love wasn't supposed to sound like a low point in your life, but without Julia by my side that's exactly what it was. I was pining for a woman that would probably most likely forget that I was even alive.

Baylor slowly removed his hand from the bar and gave me a calculating look. He opened his mouth, then snapped it shut. He then raised a brow before he finally spoke, "But you hate Julia."

"Tell me about it," I rolled my eyes. "I've heard that there was a thin line between love and hate, but when it boils down to it, that fucker was thinner than a piece of thread. It took little effort on her part before I was done for. It happened so fast I swear I didn't even have time to blink. And now," I sighed and put my head in my hands, "there may be a chance that she's pregnant, so long story short, she ran." I briefly chuckled, "She took off early and wasn't even going to say goodbye until I caught the taxi outside of your house."

"Shit, man," he cursed under his breath. "I definitely wasn't expecting all of that."

I rubbed my hand over my dark hair, "Heavy, huh? But listen, don't tell Eden for a bit, please. I don't need to chase Julia off even more."

He eyes almost bugged out of his head, "Seriously? Eden is now my wife, I don't keep things from her." I shot him a vile look, one that dared him to go there right now.

"With all due respect, this isn't about you and Eden, so can you do this one thing for me? Please?" I was begging him like a fucking pussy. I'd never once considered keeping anything from my best friend, and already I was regretting telling him about anything that went on between Julia and me.

He seemed to mull over the entire situation before I finally saw it in his eyes that he was caving. He started tearing off the edge of the wrapper of his beer, relaxing back in his seat, and said with amusement laced in his voice, "So, Julia, huh?"

"Shocked the hell out of me too. The attraction was always there, but the spark between us completely blindsided me. Now, it's like, how can I miss sleeping next to her when she was never there? I don't want to be home because it's too lonely without her. I was just a fling for her and now she wants nothing more to do with me."

"Do you honestly believe that?"

"I don't want to, no. I think she's just scared by her past. She knows that I'm not that guy but won't let herself truly believe it. Add to it the fact that she doesn't want kids."

A song cued up that served as a welcome distraction from our conversation. I turned my body so I could look towards the stage to see a twenty-something guy singing along to the song. The scene before me was utterly horrendous, but the song itself reminded me of Julia.

Without any thought as to what I was going to do next, I grabbed the collar of my suit jacket, lifting it off of the back of the stool, and dug my cellphone out of the inside pocket. Hitting the button on the side to illuminate the screen, I was disappointed to see that I had no new notifications. I knew that mostly likely she didn't even know that she had my phone number, but there were numerous social media sites she could've found me on, not to mention my law practice website. But nothing, nada. Was she even thinking about me at all? If she wasn't now, she certainly would be in a few minutes.

I opened the text messaging app and scrolled through the contacts list until I landed on the name that I had assigned for her, smiling to myself behind the meaning. While she was napping after I wore her out, I snuck her phone into the other room and input my number and then quickly called my phone from it so I would have her number as well. I felt a bit stealthy at the time, but I didn't foresee things to go down as they had.

My fingers flew across my lighted keyboard and before I lost my nerve, I hit send. Dropping my phone on the counter, I tried my best to relax in my seat, shooting glances at Baylor while trying not to wait for the moment she'd text back.

"What'd you just do?" He eyed me cautiously. Shaking my head, I wasn't going to answer that. I was too nervous as it was to see if she even replied back.

Finally, after five long minutes, my phone screen lit up, indicating one new text message.

Blonde Bombshell: Sex God? What the? Bentley?

After I read the name I stored in her phone for myself my eyes almost bugged out of my skull. I felt my fists clench into my hands and my anger quickly rising. She thought I was Bentley? Why would she associate him with sex god? Where was he? I turned my head, trying to scan the crowd of people only to see that he wasn't even here. Before I did something drastic, another text came through.

Julia: I'm only kidding, Dean. But I am changing the name in my phone. So you heard a song that reminds you of me? What is it, "Bitch" by Meredith Brooks?

She could change the name in her phone, but we still knew that what I said was true. I smiled to myself as my fingers furiously typed out my reply. The guy that couldn't carry a tune that was on stage only had one thing going for him and that was his song choice.

Me: Nice try, but no. It's "I Want You to Want Me" by Cheap Trick.

Julia: Dean...

I thought she was done and that I had messed up again. Why should I keep my feelings bottled up? I was becoming too old to play games, so I was going to take a lesson out of her book and not sugarcoat anything.

Julia: I have a song that reminds me of you. "Insane In the Brain" by Cypress Hill.

Me: Haha! Your hilarious.

Julia: You're...Mr. Smart Man, who went to school for seven years can't differentiate between your and you're?

Me: I never claimed to be an English major...

Julia: Goodnight, Dean.

I was being dismissed, but I couldn't help the spark of hope that bloomed in my chest at her actually replying to me. Perhaps, maybe I could get through to her after all. She would have to talk to me if she was pregnant, right? Then the vile thought crossed my mind that she may want to get rid of it, and I wanted to haul off and punch something for even letting the thought seep into my brain.

Of course she wouldn't do that.

But I couldn't even wholeheartedly believe it myself. I picked up my drink that had been replaced several minutes ago and swallowed the entire thing in one gulp. We had to get to the bottom of things.

Chapter 17

Julia

The past three mornings, I had woken up to a new text from Dean, each with a different song that reminded him of me.

First it was,

Dean: "Just the Way You Are," by Bruno Mars.

Then on Christmas there was,

Dean: Merry Christmas, Julia! Here is your daily dose of a song that reminds me of you, Christmas Edition. "All I Want For Christmas Is You," by Mariah Carey.

And finally, this morning was by far my favorite of all the ones he'd sent thus far,

Dean: "Justify My Love" by Madonna.

I smiled at my phone each time I saw the random song and the last one actually had me laughing out loud. He didn't seem like a Madonna guy to me, or a Mariah Carey guy for that matter. I wanted to ask if he already knew these songs or had to go on a scavenger hunt for them. Maybe he enlisted the help of Eden, but that couldn't be possible because then she'd be blowing up my phone to get the inside scoop on why I'd kept the fact that Dean and I slept together from her.

The fact that he took time out of his day just trying to reach out to me, made me fall for him just a bit more. My heart wanted me to go all in into the possibility of Dean and me. All I had to do was take a running start and cannonball my way in. But the problem was my head. It wouldn't even allow me to take the first step. Therefore, after my stomach did a happy little somersault, the scrooge had to make itself known with raging fists and come up with various excuses as to why we just couldn't happen. And even so I was grasping at straws, because they weren't even the least bit viable.

1. We lived in different states. As true as that statement was, it wasn't something that couldn't be easily remedied. There was nothing or no one truly tying me to Nashville since my best friend had moved away. I was a hair stylist, I could find work anywhere with ease.
2. He had been divorced twice. No big secret there, but then again, so had I.
3. Could I actually allow myself to love again? To be vulnerable enough to completely open my heart and soul to another man? I'd done that more than once and look where it had gotten me.

I did have to admit, that as annoying as Dean Parker could be, I actually missed his face a little bit.

Ok, a lot.

When I had gotten home from the airport, I immediately slammed my front door shut and slid my entire body down to the floor. My feet were sprawled out in front of me with one of my shoes halfway off of my heel, the contents of my purse spilling out, and my suitcase long forgotten on my front porch. I didn't care about anything. My shoulders began to forcefully shake as uncontrollable sobs racked my body. I cried harder than I ever remembered crying before. The debilitating ache in my chest hurt worse than the love my mother couldn't give me and more than any pain I suffered at the hands or mouths of my ex-husbands.

I cried for what could've been between Dean and me, if only I could completely overlook my past and misgivings.

Cried for my inability to see what the future held for myself.

And most of all, I cried for the child I may or may not be carrying and how I didn't think I could make it as a mother. It wasn't as if I had the best role model to lead by example. But, I did have my nanny, and she was such a blessing. The mother I should've had.

I sat against the door until I fell asleep, exhausted from shedding so many tears, my coat still firmly secured around my body.

The chime of my text tone pulled me out of my thoughts and I leaned forward in my stylist chair, pulling my phone from off the top of my station. My stomach did another flip when I saw that the text was from Dean.

Dean: There should be a package for you delivered at your work today. Please wait until you get home to open it and call me before you do.

No sooner did I finish reading the text and replied back with a simple, "Ok," Lisa hollered at me from the front of the Salon.

I pushed myself from my chair and made my way towards the front but I apparently wasn't walking fast enough, because she impatiently yelled, "Hey, Jules!"

I rounded the corner of the partition that separated the waiting area from the rest of the Salon, "Hold your horses!" I shouted, getting annoyed. "I can't tell if this is a place of business and relaxation with all the blasted yelling," I added with an edge of annoyance, while I looked at my receptionist, Lisa.

Placing my hands on my hips, I raised my brows, as if I was asking, *what?*

"Oh," she snapped her mouth closed, then pointed over her shoulder towards the gentleman in the dark brown uniform. "He says he has a package for you."

I took three steps towards them and glanced at the delivery man, then Lisa, then back at him, "And she couldn't sign for it?"

He quickly shook his head, "No ma'am," I flinched at the thought of actually being old enough to be called ma'am before refocusing my attention. "I have strict instructions to hand the package only to you." He thrust his electronic pad in my direction, waiting on my signature.

"Damn, Dean really wanted to make sure I received it. What the hell is it, a Faberge Egg?" I signed the small rectangle before clipping the pen back in position and handing the electronic device back to him. He proceeded to hand me a small box, about the size of a coffee mug. Heck it could really be a Faberge Egg or a coffee mug. Now I was intrigued.

I thanked the delivery man, then spun around until I was met face to face with a curious looking Lisa.

"Yeah?" I was becoming irritated with her today.

"Who's Dean and why is he sending you super-secret gifts?"

I didn't realize that I actually said his name out loud. I wanted to lie, tell her he was my accountant or something equally as probable. I didn't know exactly what he was to me and if I actually let my emotions show that I was the least bit interested in him, then it would become all too real. So, I took the pathetic way out like the coward that I was convinced I was turning into. "Curiosity killed the cat, Lisa." I stepped around her and walked back to my station, shoving the box into my purse. Out of sight, out of mind, right?

I tossed my purse and keys on my kitchen counter before grabbing my phone and the mysterious box out of the inside pocket. Placing the box in the middle of my small, round kitchen table, I took a seat and rested my chin on my forearms, eyeing it cautiously, like it was an explosive that had my name on it. The idea that he would go out of his way to send me something was perplexing. The texts were more than enough. What was in the box could be nothing to worry about, but then again it could definitely be *something*.

My mind was a jumbled mess and I was confusing myself and talking in circles.

Then came the fact that he wanted me to call him before I even opened it. I hadn't spoken to him, other than by text, in the week since I left Cottage Grove. Where I said too much and at the same time, not enough.

With the internal war raging on in my head about whether or not to call him or change my number entirely, he took the decision out of my hands. I hadn't anticipated him calling me instead.

Dean calling... flashed on my screen. Yes, I'd changed it from *Sex God*, but he should feel lucky it was his own name and not *Asshole*.

I contemplated hitting ignore and sending the call to voicemail. But the weak part of me won. I wanted to hear his voice.

"Hello," I said, after bringing the phone to my ear.

"Julia..." He responded with the low timber of his voice, then sighed. The moment I heard his voice come through my end of the phone, the dormant butterflies that had settled in my stomach began fluttering around anxiously.

"Dean," I breathed, as if his name was a natural extension of my own.

"Ah, I love it when you say my name. Although, I love it more when you scream it. Do it again," he asked. His boldness didn't have any bounds, even over the phone he had the effect to make me blush.

I couldn't stop the smile that formed on my lips. "Asshole," I muttered under my breath.

"There she is. Julia is now ready to come out and play. Be nice to a man too much and he would start to expect it. But throw in your bitchiness every now and again and he'll learn to appreciate the nicety."

Feeling the anger surge in my chest at his audacity. "Dean, I never claimed to be a *nice* person. If you want *nice*, you'll have to shop elsewhere."

"Julia, three days ago I sent you a text with a song title. It was a song that reminded me of you. What was that song?"

I didn't even have to think back to what it was, I already knew. "Just the Way You Are," I answered as I drew imaginary circles on my table with my forefinger.

"Right. I'm into you Just. The. Way. You. Are." He enunciated each individual word. "Now, did you get my gift?"

"I did," I answered as I looked up at the box. It just sat there, unmoving, mocking me.

"Did you open it?"

"You asked me not to."

"Good, go ahead and open it... if you want." He almost sounded a bit unsure of himself. Nothing like the Dean that I knew.

I drew the box towards me and cradled the phone on my shoulder. I didn't have a pair of scissors handy, which was odd even for me. I briefly considered retrieving a knife from the kitchen drawer, but I didn't want to waste any more time and I'd have it open just as fast by peeling off the tape. So I picked at the bottom edge, lifting it until I could get a good grasp on the tape and pulled it until it was completely off of the box.

I bent back the flaps and nestled inside was yet another box, this one wrapped in Christmas paper. "Ok, I've opened the box, but now I have to unwrap the actual gift." I wanted to give him some reassurance and to let him know where I was in the opening process.

"Keep going…"

The wrapping job was less than stellar, but he received extra points because I could tell he did it himself. "I almost feel bad for opening it. I didn't get you anything. But then again, I didn't buy one single Christmas present for anyone."

"Julia, that's not what this is about. I don't expect anything in return. This was just something that I wanted to do."

I ripped the paper quickly, revealing a plain white box. When I opened the flap to get to the actual gift inside, my heart lodged in my throat. My hand flew to my mouth and tears welled up in my eyes. I couldn't even begin to formulate any words, they were stuck behind my heart unable to find a way around it to break free.

Resting upon red tissue paper was a hand-painted ceramic ornament. He was recreating the tradition from my nanny… The ornament was a snowman and woman, both clad with coordinating winter hats, both with coal smiles that matched one another. And on the bottom of the snow embankment where the snow couple was perched, were the words, *"Our First Christmas 2014- Julia & Dean."*

How could my heart feel like it was healing and breaking at the same time?

"Julia?" He asked, sounding rather sad. He must've taken my silence as a negative thing. In all honesty, I didn't know it to be negative or positive.

I had to think of something to say and fast. Something that didn't confirm nor deny my love for this gift. Because I really did love it.

"This gift is rather presumptuous of you, Dean." I finally picked up the ornament and traced my fingers along the written words, where each line began and ended, the curvature of the penmanship. It was my new favorite ornament and one that I didn't think I'd ever be able to put away.

"Nah," he said, I detected a bit of playfulness in his tone before he turned serious, "I've always been a foregone conclusion. Just waiting for your head to catch up to what your heart wants."

Yeah, me too, I wanted to say. I wanted so badly to let him in, but I just couldn't break down the remainder of my walls. They were meticulously placed there for protection. But instead replied with, "Using such big words, huh?"

"Well, as you so dutifully pointed out, I did attend seven years of college. I know a big word or two."

I sighed, my voice trembling as I finally let the tears fall down my face, "Thank you. Thank you so much for this.

Chapter 18

Julia

A month has now gone by since the conversation over Dean's gift to me. We talk every now and again, but the conversations have been more and more sporadic lately since I can't express the words and feelings my heart wants to. My head was giving a whole new meaning to the word stubborn. I wanted to give him a chance, really, I did. But I would constantly be on edge, waiting for the other shoe to drop. Because being in love with me, it was inevitable that the bottom would fall out. And then where would that leave me? In even more of a heartbroken mess than I've ever been in, that's where. Dean had the power to completely wreck me and shatter the pieces to my heart. I wished they made hearts indestructible, I would be first in line for that bitch.

Every time he would call, he would all but profess his love to me, never actually coming out and saying those three words. And I would constantly dodge any bullet of expressing any feelings of my own. I was almost to the point where I wished he'd back off and go find someone who could give him everything he deserved and loved him how he should be loved. But for some reason he just wouldn't leave well enough alone.

It was almost February and at the Salon things were bustling with the upcoming Hair Show. It was every talented hair stylist's dream to have their hard work showcased. With the six stylists we had renting booths at Violet, we each had two models. On the day of the actual show, my models would have their hair colored in the richest of colors and styled in ways that were unimaginable to the everyday person. I always looked forward to the

Hair Show, but this year was an exception. I was overly tired and even more overly stressed. Dean tried calling me and I didn't even mean to snap at him. Most of the time my digs were done purposefully and this one slipped right through my lips. I could tell when he quickly bid farewell that I hurt his feelings.

I was currently cleaning up my forty-something client's neckline with my clippers, and instead of swiveling the chair, I turned my body too quickly and a wave of dizziness hit me head on. I had to brace myself on the edge of his shoulders to keep from falling over.

"Whoa," I said, pressing my hand to my chest, clearly having the wind knocked out of me. "I am so sorry," I apologized profusely, not meaning to grab ahold of his person.

He eyed me with a raised brow from the rectangular mirror that was hanging before us, "Are you all right, Julia? You are looking a bit pale."

My first instinct was to lash out asking how he could tell, my skin was already as white as it could be, but when I took a good look at my reflection, he was right. My face was completely flushed and I had deep dark purple rings stacked underneath my eyes. I prided myself in always trying to look my best, but right now I was anything but. I looked rough and that was putting it extremely mildly.

My eyes found their way back to his and his brows had knitted together inquisitively, as if he was concerned for my well-being. I flashed him my best smile and rested my hand lightly on his shoulder, "I'm fine, Dave. Just didn't get a good night's sleep last night. I'll be sure to go to bed extra early tonight." I turned the chair so I could finish up his cut and send him on his merry way.

"You must be so tired from running off all those men all the time."

I couldn't contain the laughter that bubbled from my throat, "You're funny, Dave."

I set my clippers on top of my station and took my neck duster to sweep away all the remaining little wisps of hairs, unsnapped the black cape with the custom Violet signature and ushered him to the receptionist to check out.

The possibility of being pregnant was always at the forefront of my mind. And given this bout of dizziness, along with my stress and tiredness, I knew in my heart that I was.

The thought of waiting another minute without knowing for sure put me severely on edge. I pulled out the drawer to my personal cubby at my station, grabbed my purse and keys and waved at my staff behind me as I headed for the door.

"I'll be right back," I said to Lisa at her desk before I pushed open the glass door, hearing the bell that signaled my departure.

Thirty minutes later, I had the saturated pee stick resting on the vanity in the bathroom of the Salon. I was breaking out in a sweat on my forehead and my heart was racing a mile a minute as I paced back and forth along the sand colored tile floor. Three minutes, one hundred and eighty seconds, no matter how you broke the time down it didn't seem to speed it up any.

"Crazy" by Gnarles Barkley began playing from my spilled purse in the far corner of the floor in the one person bathroom.

My ringtone for Dean.

Shit, why was he calling now?

Well, I guess there was no time like the present for him to find out the news right along with me. I bent down, grabbing the strap of my gray hobo purse, and dug around my wallet, finding the ringing contraption.

I quickly answered before bringing the phone to my ear, tentatively saying, "Hello."

"Hey, Julia," I didn't think there would ever be a time when I didn't get weak in the knees whenever I heard him breathe my name into the phone. Hearing his voice immediately made some of my nerves dissipate, but that could change within a moment's notice once the results displayed themselves.

"Dean, I think I'd be lying if I said I wasn't happy you called. I really want to apologize for flying off at you earlier. I'm tired from all this planning for the Hair Show. And that's no excuse."

"Sweetheart," I gasped hearing the term of endearment he had for me; he hadn't said it since the day I left Cottage Grove. This was just going to make things harder. He went on as if he hadn't heard the obvious hitch in my breath. "Are you sure you're feeling all right, you just voluntarily apologized to me. Wait...wait a minute!" He slightly shrieked, "You like me..."

Here we go again with that statement. I rolled my eyes, but found myself smiling, "Whatever helps you sleep at night."

I heard him release a long, drawn-out sigh, "This. Talking to you, hearing your voice through the phone helps me sleep at night. Although, I'd rather have you right next to me."

"Dean..."

"I know, I know. You don't want to hear me say things like that. But you know what, tough shit. You're going to hear me say them for as long as it takes for you to admit it to yourself that we belong together. You are a stubborn woman, but you know what? I'm just as stubborn and relentless. I am after all an attorney, I'm the worst kind of ruthless. I will stop at nothing to get what I want. And I fucking want you."

"Why?" By this time, I was leaning my free arm against the counter and tears have again welled up in my eyes. I had never been this emotional prior to meeting Dean. But everything he said, everything he did constantly pulled at my heartstrings. There was a slight tremble in my voice, "Why do you want me?"

Exasperated, he said, "Right now, I'm not even sure myself." I felt as if he had just doubled up his fist and landed it straight into my stomach. But, I had no one to blame but myself, it was my own fault. I bent my head down and squeezed my eyes shut, trying to ward off the pain in my chest. What didn't help matters was the fact that when I opened my eyes, I happened to glance over at the pregnancy test that was placed next to my hand. More than enough time had elapsed and my answer was staring at me through the little oval window.

I loathed the two pink lines, one shade darker than the other.

I took a deep breath, slowly releasing it, my anger rising and drying the tears that had formulated. "Dean, do you know what my favorite color is?" I paused for only a brief moment, before resuming, "Well, it was pink. But having these two pink lines mocking me on this pregnancy test, I'm thinking I need to change that." I couldn't help the sarcasm as it bubbled up from my chest.

"What are you?" He paused, "What are you saying, Julia?"

"I'm…I'm pregnant," I barely stumbled over the words to get them out. And once I said it aloud, it all became very real.

It finally sank in.

I could feel my heart beating stronger and faster by the second and the panic was rapidly rising in my chest. I knew that I was on the verge of an anxiety attack, but for the life of me I couldn't take slow and steady breaths. I could feel myself shutting down, wanting nothing more than to wallow in misery for how careless I had been. *What was I going to do?* I was so scared that my body was retreating into itself. Self-preservation was always my main goal and right now, it was working double time stacking back up all the bricks Dean had meticulously pulled away.

"Julia!…Julia!" I heard Dean yell through the phone.

"What?" I choked out, trying to get my heart rate back to normal by trying to take deep, even breaths.

"I said, we will figure this out. This doesn't have to be a bad thing, Julia. Having a child is a wonderful experience and I for one am glad that I get to share it with you."

No, this couldn't be happening.

I said just above a whisper, "I'm not sure I want to keep it."

A million different thoughts were racing through my head, resulting in a sharp throb at my temples. I needed to go lie down.

"You're certainly not aborting it!" He roared.

"Dean, I'm a bitch, I'm not fucking heartless," I snapped.

"You could've fooled me," he sighed, but I could almost feel his anger towards me seeping through the earpiece on the phone. "Call me when you're done acting like a child." He viciously retorted, then promptly hung up on me.

It didn't matter to me where I was at the moment, I sank to my knees on the floor of the bathroom in the Salon and allowed my tears to break free. So many emotions were running rampant through my body; I was confused, ashamed, lonely, but most of all I was scared that I finally ran Dean off for good. *That was what I wanted, right?*

A heavy pounding on the door rattled me from my daze. My mouth felt like glue and I didn't know if I'd actually be able to speak. Swallowing a few times, I tried to sound lighthearted and that nothing was wrong, but I ended up croaking out, "Yeah?"

"Jules, you ok in there?" Lisa asked, her voice floating through the door, sounding muffled against the wood.

I thought about my options, I could clean myself up and go back to work as if nothing happened or I could just go home. Pulling my blankets high over my head sounded better than anything else at the moment.

"No, actually I'm not feeling too well. I think I'm going to head home and get some rest."

"Ok, babe." I saw the shadow from her feet under the door move away so I knew that the coast was currently clear, but there was no chance in hell that I could slip out of the Salon undetected. I was going to have to clean up.

I curved my hands around the top of the vanity and managed to pull myself into a standing position. That little bit of exertion took way more effort than it should have. I was emotionally spent and drained of every last bit of feeling I had. I closed my eyes and lifted my chin, then only peeked with one eye towards the mirror. I didn't want the wreckage of my face to hit me all at once, but once I saw my reflection staring back at me both eyes automatically flew open. My cheeks were stained with tears and black mascara streaks. My makeup was now haphazardly all over my face and my eyes puffy and swollen. To top it off, I had red hives covering my chest above my shirt from my anxiety attack.

Reaching for the faucet, I turned the water on to as warm as I could stand it and began bringing handfuls of liquid to my face so I could clean away most of the evidence. My fingertips alone weren't scrubbing much of my mascara away, so I reluctantly opted for the rough brown paper towels. After going through a few of them, getting just the edges wet and scrubbing my face, all of my makeup was officially gone. But now in its place was long red streaks from the scratchiness of the towel on my skin.

I snatched my purse up off the floor quickly, dangling it along beside me, threw open the door and rushed out the building with my head steadily pointed towards the floor. I always held my head up high, no matter what I was doing. Walk of shame the next morning in the same clothes, I owned that with my resting bitch face in place, daring someone to snicker. But this,

I couldn't do it. I left my dignity on the floor of that bathroom and I didn't know if I would ever be able to recover.

Once I let myself inside the front door of my house, I quickly glanced at my mail that I had retrieved before throwing it on my dining room table, several envelopes scattering across the wooden surface. Then I kicked my shoes off in the hallway, pulled back my blankets on my bed and crawled inside where I slept for several hours.

I didn't realize until later that one of the envelopes that was among the rest of my unopened mail on my table was from Riverbend Maximum Security Institution in Nashville. It seemed as if Logan Wesson was being released early...

Chapter 19

Dean

"Mr. Parker, your three o'clock is here." Bea informed me, her hand poised on the doorknob and her face angled just barely inside the door. No matter how many times I insisted that she call me Dean, it was still Mr. Parker. Always business with her.

I was casually leaning back in my chair allowing my elbow to rest on my mahogany desk, deep thoughts running through my mind. I was thinking about everything and nothing at the same time. I believed that I had maintained this same exact position for the past two hours since getting off the phone with Julia.

She was pregnant with my child...Finally, I had the chance to become a father and Julia wanted nothing to do with either of us.

I was hopeful that at some point in time, sooner rather than later would be nice, she would warm up to the idea of *us*. I knew that I was already deep in her heart, she was just too afraid to admit it. But would there ever be a possibility of her actually being open to the idea of a baby?

I'd been privy to glimpses of the kindhearted person that Julia could be and I had no doubt or fear that she wouldn't be a terrific mother. She knew firsthand what it felt like to not be wanted by a parent, so I'd imagine she wouldn't want that for her own child. Ultimately that's *her* greatest fear; that she wouldn't be good enough.

These weren't the most ideal circumstances, but I wanted nothing more than to have Julia by my side; I had wanted it the moment I laid eyes on her. I wanted to be there for her and the baby every step of the way.

Pressing the heel of my hand into the middle of my chest, I hoped that it would alleviate some of the pain I felt.

I shouldn't have gone off on her the way I did, but she knew each proper step it took to push my buttons.

"Dean!" Bea hollered, now using my first name. When I focused back on my surroundings, she was completely in the room, standing right in front of me, her hand waving around in my face. She had a scowl set firmly in place and her lips were pursed together. This was Bea seriously agitated. I never wanted to see a look that lethal directed at me again.

"What?" I barked, sitting up straight in my chair and readjusting my tie, trying to seem as if she didn't scare the ever-loving shit out of me. Even though she was my secretary, being the mother figure to me that she was, I didn't ever want to piss her off. And I had. Big time.

"Your three o'clock has been waiting for ten minutes," she bit out each word slowly with precision and annoyance. Flinging my hand in the direction of the door, I was signaling to her both that she was dismissed and to send my new client in.

Rising from my chair, I lifted my black suit jacket off of the back, and slipped my arms into the sleeves. Then I finished by pushing the only two buttons through their holes and smoothed out the wrinkles. I was ready to get this consultation over with so I could head home.

This day couldn't possibly get any worse.

Lord, did I wish that statement were true.

I casually leaned against my desk before straightening up when I saw the door knob turn, I shouldn't have ignored the overwhelming feeling of dread that I felt at that precise moment. I should've hightailed it out the window; my office *was* on the first floor, so it would've been easy enough. Or I could've hidden in the closet, anything to get away from this moment.

The first thing I noticed as the woman let herself into my office were the four-inch stiletto heels that reminded me so much of the ones Julia flaunted around in. And they were red...The color of love. The color of lust. The color of sin. The color of death.

My gaze traveled up the pair of long, toned legs that disappeared at the knee under a black pencil skirt. I skimmed to her small waist and correction; she was wearing a dress rather than a skirt. An incredibly enticing little black dress that scooped at the neckline, showcasing ample cleavage. Her breasts weren't as full as Julia's and honestly didn't even compare. That is how I knew that I was head over heels in love with Julia, I compared her to every other woman, and no one even held a candle to the beauty of her.

The woman's dark brown hair was loosely curled around her shoulders, and when I got to her lips my blood ran cold as my heart slammed in my chest, and my once-appreciative gaze narrowed.

I knew those lips, the bottom thin and the top just slightly plump. And now they parted with a sadistic smirk. Hell, once upon a time I had loved those fucking lips. I wouldn't let my eyes travel any further, because those lips were connected to a face that I didn't ever want to see again. I didn't want to give her the satisfaction of garnering my attention. That face housed what I once found was an incredible set of milk chocolate-brown eyes that I spent hours getting lost in.

Her mouth parted to speak and she ran her tongue along her bottom lip, "Hello, Dean," she said, in that voice that had once sounded like honey to me and could've easily brought me to my knees. Now, it sounded like nails on a chalkboard; harmful to my ears and hazardous to my health.

I gruffly cleared my throat before I reluctantly allowed my eyes to snap to those of my ex-wife... "Kate."

166

No other formal introductions needed to take place, so I turned my back on her and dropped into my chair. There was no doubt in my mind that I needed to be sitting down for this conversation. "Please have a seat," I gestured towards one of the open chairs positioned in front of my desk. Once she got herself situated, a little too provocatively for my liking, I rolled my eyes, then asked as if I was bored, "To what do I owe this pleasure?"

She looked down at her hands that were clasped together in her lap, "Mark left me and Aiden. I found out he was cheating on me."

I automatically barked out a laugh, this was rich. "Didn't see that one coming, huh?"

Her eyes snapped to mine, "Dear, that's not fair."

"Isn't it though? It seems as if karma is knocking on your doorstep." I crossed my arms in front of my chest, "Sucks, doesn't it?"

Her voice got really small, "You were always working and were never around."

Seriously? Making me to blame once again. I needed to know why the hell she was here so she could hurry up and be on her merry little way. The onslaught of a tension headache was forming between my eyes and her presence was only making it worse. I squeezed my eyes shut as I pressed my fingers on the bridge of my nose trying to get the pain to lessen. "What are you doing here, Kate? If you're here to dredge up the past and place blame solely on me again, you can get your ass out of my chair and out of my office." My voice was growing steadily louder the more I spoke.

Her face fell; not once in the entire time that we were together did she ever hear me raise my voice. Maybe that's one place we went wrong, I gave in to her every whim and never ever put my foot down. We never fought. Maybe that's why I desired Julia so much, she pushed me until I fought with her. It's not healthy to be a pushover and that's exactly what I was with Kate. So, in many ways Kate helped me, she forced me to analyze my past relationships and make sure that I didn't make the same mistakes again.

She squared her shoulders and took a deep breath, channeling all of her courage, "I want you to represent me in my divorce."

This time I released a laugh from deep within my gut. "When did you become such a comedian?" Her eyes narrowed into slits, which just caused me to laugh harder. Once I was finally able to catch my breath and speak without laughing, I glared into those eyes of her and deadpanned, "No."

"Excuse me?" she scoffed with an attitude.

"You heard me. N-O. I reserve every right to refuse a client and right now, you are on top of that list."

And if Julia ever had impeccable timing, this certainly wasn't it. My phone lit up and started skittering across my desk. I quickly silenced it because I didn't have time for another fight at the moment, but it instantly lit up again with her calling.

I raised a finger towards Kate without even looking up from my phone as I pressed the screen to take the call. The thought of it being an emergency crossed my mind; she wouldn't have called back unless it was.

"Yeah?" I answered, trying my best to sound undistracted but with Kate in front of me, things were a bit tense and uncomfortable and I knew Julia could immediately sense that.

"Dean?" She sounded so small and fragile, completely unlike the Julia I knew. "Is it possible for someone to be released from jail even if they haven't served a fraction of their sentence?"

What the hell? She called me repeatedly to ask me a hypothetical question? And one that wasn't even in my direct field? I responded, mustering up the most businesslike tone that I could without sounding too exasperated, "Julia, I'm not a criminal lawyer. Divorce is my direct level of expertise, but I suppose he could if he appealed and won or if he got credit for good behavior."

"Dean, I'm still here," Kate muttered, her tone annoyed. I looked up from my desk and found her with her arms crossed in front of her and a scowl set firmly in place. I had honestly forgotten she was even there.

"Kate, give me a minute, please."

"Kate? As in your ex-wife, Kate?" Julia asked through the phone, her voice taking on a terse tone.

I went completely quiet because I knew what it must sound like to her. I brought my free hand to my temple and begin to rub along the skin with my fingers in clockwise circles. I sighed and shook my head, before I responded with a simple, "Yes."

Dejected, Julia said, "I see. Well, I'm sorry to have bothered you. Please don't let me tie you up any further."

"Julia, wait..." I tried to interject, but she had already hung up.

"Dammit," I screamed as I slammed my hand down on the top of my desk, making a few items rattle on the surface from the action.

I stood up and stalked my way to my closed office door, yanking it open by the handle. "Out!" I forced out through my clenched teeth.

Kate had turned around in her seat, her eyes wide and mouth agape. "You can't be serious?"

"As a fucking heart attack, Kate. You wasted your time and mine by coming here. Now, you need to leave."

The stress and effect of the entire day was weighing heavily on my shoulders and I wanted nothing more than to drown myself in some heavy liquor and possibly even hit something. I wondered if I could get Bentley to volunteer himself as my own personal punching bag.

Kate hadn't moved an inch, was she testing me? I had no problem escorting her ass out of my office myself, but I knew that Bea would frown heavily upon that. And I didn't feel like having to deal with the police department and explaining my circumstance; I think I'd had enough shit to last me a good long while.

"NOW!" I screamed so loud that I felt my voice grow hoarse and my throat felt scratchy. The alcohol I was looking forward to would only further enhance the burn.

That finally got her attention though, so she stood up, threw her purse over her shoulder and shuffled out as fast as she could. I followed after her, only stopping at the edge of the reception area. I braced my hands along the window pane, glaring through the glass to make sure she left the premises entirely. Only when I couldn't see the reflection of the tail lights on her car any longer did I finally breathe a sigh of relief and hang my head.

I had been awarded my chance to go off on Kate and while it felt glorious I couldn't help the feeling that I had hurt Julia even further in the process. I needed to go home and cool off, but first thing in the morning Julia was going to listen to what I had to say. About everything. All of my cards were going to be laid out on the table. I was done messing around. I was going to claim what was mine.

"Ahem," Bea cleared her throat from her desk behind me. *Fuck.* Now was I going to have to endure the wrath of my secretary too? I really didn't want to have to fire her, only to end up calling and groveling for her to come back tomorrow.

I pushed myself off of the window and turned around only to see a bottle of elite bourbon perched on the edge of her desk and Bea with a smirk and a raised brow. "I'll remember never to piss you off," she chuckled.

"Funny thing, I was thinking the same thing about you before you let Kate into my office." I walked over and placed my hand around the neck of the bottle, dragging it off the desk until it was resting against my side. "Now I'm thinking that I need to formulate a plan of retaliation against you.

But the bourbon is a great start for an apology." lifted the bottle in the air. "And I don't even want to know why you have an expensive bottle of bourbon stashed away here at work."

"I take it that was someone who you aren't on the best terms with?"

"Ex-wife *numero dos*. She's never allowed to set foot back in here." I scratched my head as my mind wandered. "Why she traveled from Texas to Oregon to see if I would represent her in her divorce I'll never know." I shrugged my shoulders, "Nor do I really care." I shuffled my feet into my office, suddenly feeling as if I had been hung out to dry, to retrieve my briefcase before I left for the day. I hollered over my shoulder, "Bea, go home to that husband of yours. I'll see you in the morning."

I drove home without facing any other infractions and decided to forgo the drinking and just face planted onto my mattress with my clothing all still in place. I stayed in the same exact position with my nose scrunched up in the sheets until morning and the first signs of dawn trickled through my blinds waking me up.

Chapter 20

Dean

It was Saturday and I hadn't heard from Julia in several days. Even after the numerous messages I left her groveling and begging for her to listen to me, my calls remained unanswered. She completely shut me out and I hated it. I swallowed my pride and put aside my reservations about sounding like a stalker and resorted to trying to get ahold of her at Violet. It was a dead end. They told me she was taking a few days off due to illness so she could rest up. There was nothing that I myself could do since we lived several thousand miles apart, so I sent her flowers with a message to feel better and to call me.

Lounging on my couch with my head resting against the back cushion and my hand tapping along on the arm, I came to the conclusion that I was extremely bored. My mind was wandering in a thousand different ways and I needed to focus my attention on something else. I hadn't been over to bug Eden and Baylor in a while and I missed Norah something fierce, so I trekked out through my yard to theirs so I could hassle The Jenkinses.

Going through their open garage, which indicated to me that they were home, I let myself in through the laundry room and was instantly greeted by Norah.

"Hey, Norah Bean," I exclaimed, genuinely happy to see her.

She finished throwing the wet clothes in her hands into the dryer, then threw herself into my arms giving me a big hug. "Uncle Dean! It feels like I haven't seen you in forever!" She continued to brace onto me and I had no other choice but to feel guilty at her remark. My dealing with my problems was no excuse to making Norah feel neglected.

"Oh sweetie, I'm so sorry. We'll have to go out on an ice cream date later tonight. How does that sound?" I asked, ruffling up her blonde hair at the top of her head. She hated it when I did that which just further pushed me to do it every time I saw her.

"Ugh," she whined, pushing off of me and running her fingers through her long straight locks, trying to comb through all of the tangles. "That sounds like fun but stop doing that. I am twelve years old now, I can beat you up."

She was adorable and would always be my little Norah Bean. But standing there with the scowl on her face and her little hip protruding out with her hand resting on it, she was every bit of the teenager with an attitude. And the kicker was, she wasn't even technically considered a teen yet. I felt a twinge of sympathy for Baylor and Eden, they were going to have their hands full with this one. I couldn't help but chuckle at her thinking that she could beat me up. "You do realize that I'm 6'5", you can't even jump and reach my head, little shrimp. Is your dad making you do laundry?"

I just made situations worse and made her even more aggravated by calling her a shrimp, but it was hilarious to poke fun at her. She rolled her eyes, "No, it was Eden. Part of my chores." Then shrugging a shoulder, she added, "It's not so bad now that she explained each step for me. Dad did a basic run through and I ended up throwing one of Eden's red shirts into the washer and turned all of our whites pink. Ask dad about his pink underwear," Norah snickered.

And on that note, I turned on my heel and threw over my shoulder, "Yeah, I'll pass," and walked into the kitchen where Baylor was sitting on a barstool at the island and Eden was slaving away at the stove. I walked over to Eden first, sticking my head over the stove and lifting the lids to scope out what was cooking in each pot. I then leaned down and gave Eden a kiss on the cheek, "Hey," I said.

"Hey yourself, stranger."

"I know...I know...I haven't been around much lately," I made a detour to the fridge, stopping to bend down and scratch Petunia on the head, noting her deep growl. I grabbed a beer and lifted it to Baylor with a raised brow, silently asking if he needed another. He lifted his chin in the affirmative so I went back in and grabbed another, then sat down next to him at the bar. Twisting off the cap and taking a long pull, I grimaced before setting it down on the countertop. "Damn, I should've brought a Bud Light from the house, these Heinekens taste like shit."

"No one is forcing you to drink it, asshole," Baylor muttered as he took a swig of his beer of choice.

"Touché. Yeah, I just got the 'you're never around' inquisition from Norah as we talked laundry. Speaking of which," I pointed to Baylor, "I now know you're sporting pink panties." I winked as I lifted my beer to my mouth for another drink, forcing myself to swallow it down. Damn, I really should've just gotten a bottle of water.

Baylor's sharp elbow instantly met my ribcage. "Fuck man, what was that for?" I frowned, while rubbing at my throbbing side.

Eden turned around with a spatula in one hand and the other on her hip, "Boys, play nice or I'll put you two in time out."

"Sorry, babe," Baylor apologized with his beer to his lips. I could see the smile forming from behind the bottle. He was so frigging whipped it wasn't even funny. It was good to see the two of them happy though.

"Yeah, yeah, sorry Eden," I muttered. "Oh, before I forget, I'm kidnapping your daughter for ice cream tonight. Hey, Eden, have you heard from Julia lately?" I knew most likely that she didn't know about the two of us since I haven't gotten an earful from her, but I had to dig around to see how she was doing.

Baylor eyed me intently from his seat and Eden replied, "You know, it has been a few days since I've heard from her. Last time I talked to her she said she was sick with a bug or something. So I ordered her to load up on vitamin C and rest up. She works herself too much." She raised a brow in my direction, "Why do you want to know?"

"Oh, you know," I tried playing it off, but kept an eye on Baylor's reactions. If he made even the most obvious of movements, he would completely blow my cover. "Just seeing if she misses our verbal jabbing sessions. I must admit, my life has been pretty uneventful since she left and I can't fight with anyone."

Eden's expression turned grim, and she said as she placed her hand over her chest, "Oh Dean. I feel so awful, here Baylor and I have each other and you don't have anyone." Oh no, I didn't like the direction that this conversation was heading. This had definitely escalated quickly and I hadn't even foreseen it happening. If she said 'Bless your heart' next I was out of there.

"You're lonely, that's why you haven't been over here much. Because we are throwing our newlywed status in your face." By that point my eyes were bugging out of my head and my grip was tightening on my beer bottle. Baylor was chuckling it up over from his chair, enjoying the laugh at my expense. She snapped her fingers as if she just had the best idea ever. "We'll have to get you set up on a date. Maybe even a *blind* date." She looked from Baylor, who was now laughing hysterically, over to me and the stoic expression I was sporting. She was actually fucking serious. "I know!" her face lit up like a kid on Christmas morning, "Maisie! She seems like a *sweet girl*," she forced herself to spit out, "if you go for that sort of, desperate flaunting that she seems to have going on. But, hey, she seems like the type to be a sure thing," she wagged her eyebrows up and down.

My mouth was hanging wide open, I couldn't believe she would even have the audacity to suggest the town tramp. Once I got over my stunned silence, I looked towards the ceiling to ask for the strength I needed to get through the rest of this bizarre conversation. "Yeah, Maisie and I will *never* happen. *Ever*. I don't even think Bentley would go there and he chases everything." I held up my hand in Baylor's direction, "No offense, dude," referring to the time he made out with Maisie. In his defense though, he was terribly drunk. I couldn't let her think that she could set me up with someone because I knew it would ultimately end up getting back to Julia during one of their conversations. I had to put the kibosh on this immediately.

I awkwardly cleared my throat, "I'm actually already seeing someone," I said matter-of-factly before I thought about rephrasing my statement. I started paying a little too much attention to my beer bottle, twirling it around on the counter. "Ok, well *seeing* isn't the correct terminology," I smiled to myself at my use of a 'big' word, Julia would be proud. "I'm interested in someone. *Greatly interested*." I focused my eyes back on Eden, who stood there relatively unmoving with a cocked brow. She was sizing up my answer and judging to see if I was blowing smoke in her face to get her off of my back. I flashed a full, genuine smile, pulling out all the stops and even showing off my pearly whites.

"Ok," she said before revealing a smile of her own.

My answer seemed to suffice and mollify her for the time being. She turned her attention back towards the stove and whatever she was cooking. I was in the clear, I almost felt the need to wipe the sweat off of my brow that had formed at dodging that bullet. She didn't even try to pry who I was interested in out of me.

I tipped the corner of my mouth up in a triumphant smirk, but then Baylor snickered and cleared his throat...

Fuck.

I shook my head curtly and glared at him, my hands forming into fists under the counter.

He wouldn't dare.

"So, who's the girl, Dean?" He asked the question with an air of nonchalance as he casually lifted his beer to his lips.

I turned and watched horrified as Eden sat down her spoon in the center of the stove and started turning back around towards us.

Sweat was now dotting along my forehead in abundance as time seemed to be moving in slow motion. There was only so much fabrication of the truth I could take. The pressure was too much and I was going to break and automatically blurt out, *Julia*. I just knew it. Then all the dominoes already in place would come toppling down and ruin everything I had worked for. I would be fielding monotonous question after question all night with no end in sight...

When did this happen?

How did it happen?

What are your intentions?

Then the death threats would come, not from just Eden, saying that if I hurt Julia that she would rip my dick off and feed it to Petunia. And that damn dog hated me enough to do it out of spite. But then the threats from Julia would begin to pour in because I had blabbed like a little girl over our trysts.

She would hate me and I would be reduced to a puddle of nothing and have my man card stripped clean for actually shedding tears.

Eden pissed off was bad enough, I had witnessed that inner rage of hers firsthand when she went off on Baylor's first bitch of a wife, Kristina. But Eden and Julia together? That was diabolical and I was petrified.

All of this obsessive inner dialogue wasn't necessary because I was saved by Eden's phone vibrating on their kitchen table. She quickly wiped her hands off on a dish towel and walked over to retrieve it.

Thank God.

This left me plenty of time to rip Baylor a brand new asshole. I snapped my head to him and reared my arm back, getting myself ready to throw one helluva punch, when something Eden said caught my attention.

Her brows knitted together, "Yes, I'm friends with Julia Caldwell." She moved back over to the other side of the island, facing us. I was already on instant alert once Julia's name was mentioned. "I'm listed as her emergency contact?" I stood abruptly, almost knocking over the barstool with the backs of my thighs. I lowered my arm and gripped the underside of the edge of the countertop as my heart rate increased.

Emergency contact?

What the hell was wrong? And why couldn't I hear the other end of the conversation?

Eden's stance immediately changed, turning rigid before she began trembling, bringing her hand towards her, placing it against her forehead. Baylor was out of his chair and behind Eden in an instant, placing his hands on her shoulders for support.

I was going out of my mind with worry. Eden hadn't spoken another word, but had started chewing on her bottom lip. That was one of her nervous habits. I wasn't liking this one bit.

"Ok, so she's at the Vanderbilt University Medical Center?" Her voice was cracking and I could see tears well up in her eyes.

My grip tightened on the counter, so hard that my fists began to throb. I needed answers and I needed them now.

"Yes, I know where it's located. I'll be taking the first flight out I can get." Complete sadness and worry etched on her face, which had me scared. I was scared that Julia had been hurt badly. And the baby...my heart dropped in my chest.

"No," she shook her head, "she doesn't have any other family. Yes, thank you." Eden moved the phone away from her ear and ended the call. Julia did have family, she had me, it was just that no one else knew that. But that was about to change right fucking now.

Eden was looking at the granite countertop, not really focusing on anything. She allowed the tears to break free anc they were steadily streaming down her face.

I had to take a deep breath; my heart was frantically beating against my ribs and I couldn't help the gut-wrenching feeling that my world was going to come crumbling down around me.

Eden just stood there in an unmoving daze and I wanted nothing more than to shake her in order for her to spit out what had happened. But I backed off because I knew that Baylor would have my ass.

She finally began relaying what was said to her on the phone. "They said that her neighbor heard her screaming and when they arrived they found her unconscious." She paused and my mind instantly jumped to the worst-case scenarios. What if she was having a miscarriage?

This was all my fault.

I instinctively came around the sland, inching my way towards her. "She hasn't regained consciousness but they said," a sob broke free, "she has numerous bruises and lacerations. It didn't look like anyone forced their way into her house, but she was beaten pretty badly. The extent of her injuries aren't known yet." She looked around at the stove, then back to the countertop, "I need to get ready to leave."

My vision was hazy and then I could only see red. I needed more answers.

I pounded my fist on the countertop, the thud echoing throughout the kitchen, causing Baylor's attention to set on me. Through my clenched jaw, I ground out, "I'm coming with you."

Her gaze snapped to mine in my peripheral, "What? Why?"

Staring at the cabinets but not really seeing them, I cracked my knuckles. "Did they say anything about the baby?"

"What baby?" she shrieked.

Now I was looking directly at her, my tone almost to the point of being menacing, but dammit, I was pissed. "My baby!"

Her eyes bulged out of her head. She was truly shocked; not only at my outburst, but because of the bomb I just dropped. "What the hell are you talking about?"

I surged forward and grasped her by her shoulders, "The baby that Julia and I are having together."

Eden looked over towards Baylor who was still standing next to her and he instantly frowned.

"There is no time to place blame on who did or did not tell you what was happening. We have to get to Julia."

An hour later, Eden and I were lucky enough to catch the redeye to Nashville. The airfare was astronomical but I didn't even blink when I thrust my American Express card in the ticket agent's face. We boarded the plane with only seconds to spare and I had just tightened my seatbelt, settling in for the flight. My nerves were shot, I was on the verge of tears, and my damn leg wouldn't quit bouncing up and down no matter how much I concentrated on making it stop.

Eden had her arms crossed in front of her and she had yet to speak to me or even give me the satisfaction of looking my way since Baylor had dropped us off at the airport. This was her being way more than just pissed, she was hurt and I now was burdened to carry that guilt on my shoulders as well.

Sure, it was our business but Julia was her best friend and I was sure it was twisting Eden up inside that she hadn't confided in her.

I couldn't help but think of how I had never outright told Julia that I loved her. But I did, I loved her so fucking much that it hurt. I had to rub the heel of my palm into the center of my chest just to try and alleviate some of the constant pain that consumed me.

The fact that I loved her was more than implied, but I had waited for her to catch up with me before I said the three words. And all for what? Now there was the uncertain possibility that I might never get to say them at all.

Stop thinking like that. Try to keep positive.

But it was no use, every possible scenario scanned through my brain and I kept coming back to the same pragmatic outcome.

Then something hit me. The vague call I had received from her the other day. Things were tense and I was distraught with thoughts of her not keeping the baby and then with Kate appearing, I never gave her question a second thought.

"Is it possible for someone to be released from jail even if they haven't served a fraction of their sentence?"

"Logan," I blurted out, bracing my arms on the rests and leaning forward until my back was completely off the seat. "It had to have been Logan."

Eden shifted in her seat, "What do you know about Logan?" Her tone was accusing but I just ignored it.

"I know that he abused her. But then she called me the other day and was extremely vague asking about if people could get off early for good behavior. She must've had Logan put in jail." God, how could I have been so stupid? I wanted to punch the seat in front of me for the overwhelming mix of anger and guilt I felt, but I didn't need to land *my* ass in jail.

Her face instantly paled, "He abused her? She told you that? She's never told me that..." Eden pulled her bottom lip in between her teeth as it trembled.

I nodded and my voice went soft, "I love her, Eden." She needed to know that this wasn't a competition to find out who knew the most about Julia.

"She must love you too. She obviously doesn't tell just anyone about her past," the underlying hurt in her voice was just too much and I could detect a twinge of jealousy.

Resting my head on the top of the seat, I sighed... "I thought that she did...Love me, but now I'm not really sure. I just have to know for myself that she's all right."

Glancing out the window into the dark of night, I prayed that both she and the baby were all right...

Everything *had* to be ok.

The cab came to a halt in the half-circle entrance of the Emergency Room. I threw a handful bills that equaled more than enough for our fare through the center partition at the cabbie. It was still the dead of night as Eden and I rushed in through the automatic glass doors with only our coats on our backs. We didn't know what Julia's condition would be but packing a bag would've taken up precious minutes and it wasn't high on our list of priorities at the time.

The waiting room was fairly empty, so Eden walked straightaway to the large wooden reception desk that dominated the area. The lady behind the desk smiled politely, "May I help you?"

Eden placed her arms on top of the chest-high desk, "I'm Eden Richardt, I was notified that my friend Julia Caldwell was here."

A few clicks on her keyboard and she was nodding in confirmation, "Yes, Ms. Richardt, I will just need to verify with some identification please."

Eden began rummaging around her purse, pulling out her wallet. She struggled to remove her driver's license from the plastic divider. Finally she pulled it free and handed it over to the receptionist. "Here you go, but it has my married name of Jenkins. I got married a few months ago."

The receptionist glanced at the ID and returned it to her, smiling, "Congratulations on your marriage."

I rolled my eyes and internally groaned at their niceties. We were here for Julia, not to become best friends.

The receptionist stood and edged towards the end of her desk. "Right this way, I'll take you to her room." We each began following her until she glanced back and noticed I was coming as well. She shook her head, "Sir, I'm sorry, I can't allow you back there. Mrs. Jenkins is only authorized because she's her emergency contact. You'll have to wait out here."

Say what?

My defenses were up and I was more than ready to give her a piece of my mind until Eden turned around and placed her hand on my forearm. Sympathy swimming in her eyes, she said, "I'll come back out when I find out anything."

As soon as she removed her hand, I was left to my own devices. I glanced around, eyeing the numerous empty chairs and I knew I wouldn't be able to sit still. Knowing that Julia was just mere feet away and not knowing what her current condition was, I began to pace. Back and forth along the linoleum floor until an officer stopped directly in my path.

"Mr. Parker?" I looked up and nodded, acknowledging my name. "Mrs. Jenkins said that you may have some knowledge pertaining to what happened with Miss Caldwell."

Crossing my arms in front of my chest, I explained what I knew, which ultimately wasn't much. "Julia's ex-husband Logan. That's the first direction you should take. I don't know his last name, but I do know he

183

abused her in the past. She called me the other day asking if someone could be released from jail early." When he gave me a quizzical expression, I replied, "I'm a lawyer, although only a divorce lawyer, but she thought I might know the answer. If she helped send him to jail and he got out, there may have been some retaliation on his end." Bile rose up in the back of my throat with having to actually voice my thoughts out loud.

After a few more questions, the officer said he would return in the morning after Julia was able to get some rest.

I took this to be good news and to mean that Julia was actually awake.

An hour later, Eden emerged from behind the closed doors, her cheeks stained with tears and her arms wrapped around herself. Seeing her look so upset had the bottom falling out of my stomach. I flat-out sprinted across the room until I was standing right in front of her. I braced my hands on her shoulders and crouched down until I was looking directly into her sad eyes, no match for my frantic ones.

"What's wrong?"

She managed a small smile, "It was just so hard seeing her larger-than-life persona lying in a hospital bed so fragile. She's asking to see you, they are wanting to do an ultrasound to check on the baby." I blanched, not yet used to being associated with a baby.

"How is she doing?" I wanted to find out for myself and I would, but first I needed to be able to brace myself for the worst.

"She's pretty banged up." She released a humorless laugh, "worried about her appearance."

"Sounds like Julia to me. But I don't care about that, I just want her and the baby to be all right."

She stared into my eyes for a moment before saying, "You really care about her, don't you?"

"Eden, I already told you that I love her." I paused a moment and placed my hands on my hips. "She's it for me. I now realize that my first two marriages were just gearing me up for the whirlwind that is Julia Caldwell. Now I need to convince that stubborn, hardheaded woman that I'm not going anywhere. Ever."

"You know she'll fight you every step." She didn't pose this as a question but a statement, because we both knew it was absolutely true.

I began walking towards the doors that would hopefully lead me to my future and I stopped to look back over my shoulder to Eden. "I wouldn't have it any other way."

"Go on," she mouthed then held up her cell phone, "I'm going to call Baylor, fill him in."

I took a deep breath and made the walk down the long white corridor towards my entire life.

Chapter 21

Julia

I was finally able to open my eyelids. It was just a sliver but enough to be accosted by bright white fluorescent lights.

Where was I?

I could just faintly make out the outline of a woman hovering over me out of one eye. Moving my hands around beneath me, I felt less-than-desirable sheets beneath me. *I was in a bed? Was I in the hospital?* My head was pounding and I had no other choice but to flinch as the thumping continued between my ears.

"Water," I spoke around the feeling of cotton lodged deep in my throat. It came out as more of a croak due to the hoarseness of my tone.

"Julia?"

That was Eden. I knew that voice anywhere.

My head snapped to the side, where the sound of her voice was coming from. Craning my neck caused more pain to radiate throughout my body. I winced again due to the debilitating discomfort.

I felt tentative fingers stroke my skin before her soft hand engulfed my own, giving it a gentle squeeze. I struggled to open my eyes but could only get my right one to cooperate.

"Eden?"

Another gentle squeeze followed by a brief sob, "Yeah, Jules. I'm here, Dean too."

A strangled cry released from my lips. "Dean's here?"

"Oh Jules, he's out of his mind with worry. Not to say that I'm not, but I've never seen him like this before. They wouldn't let him back here with me though since he wasn't listed on any of the paperwork. So I'm sure he's giving them hell out in the waiting room."

He came for me?

My hand pulled free and instinctively I reached up to feel my stomach.

Our baby.

"Jules, why didn't you tell me? We're best friends and I thought you told me everything."

I felt a tear fall from my eyes and travel down my cheek at the sadness in her tone. She was hurt that I hadn't confided in her. But how could I?

"I didn't want to believe it myself. Everything happened so quickly. I vowed never to fall in love again but I wasn't expecting Dean Parker to come barging in. He makes it hard to say no to him. I find myself not wanting to."

The nurse came back up and began poking and prodding around on my arm that housed an IV line. "Julia, do you know why you're here?" She asked in almost a condescending tone that I wasn't really appreciating at the moment. "You were the victim of an attack. You were unconscious for quite a while."

That one word had everything surging back to me, clear as day.

Victim.

That was the same exact word the jail had used when they notified me of Logan's release. As the *victim*, it was their duty to inform me of his impending departure. Making it sound as if he was leaving the country rather than getting released early of his own recognizance.

I wasn't a fucking *victim*, I was a *survivor*...

Victims didn't fight back against their attacker.

Victims didn't live to fucking tell about it.

I remembered moping around my house over the next few days after learning about the pregnancy, really thinking through all my options. I wouldn't even answer my phone because I needed to clear my head and didn't need the extra added distractions.

Then there was the fact that Dean's ex-wife had re-entered the picture for some ungodly reason and it caused my jealousy to spike.

I didn't like caring for someone so deeply that I let jealousy get the best of me.

But there I was instantly shoving Dean into the same category as Logan and Paul, when I shouldn't have. That wasn't fair to him when he didn't do anything to warrant it. I didn't even let him explain his side of the story before I began jumping to conclusions.

He wouldn't do that do me and had shown me on numerous occasions that he genuinely cared for me. I didn't deserve him.

My doorbell rang later in the afternoon and the thought of peeking through my side window to see who it was didn't occur to me until after I yanked open my storm door.

Logan stood before me, my screen door opened and resting behind his back, so he was halfway into my house before I even knew what was happening. Pushing his way into my space, just like old times. Typical Logan.

I took three giant steps backwards, trying to get away from him, but his large frame continued to advance, making it difficult to proceed any further. I felt my heart rate increase but I tried to keep my breathing even so I wouldn't let him know that he affected me in any little way.

That's what he fed off of, fear, he lived for it.

Seeing someone else wither away in front of him out of fear from his demanding and malevolent persona. I was a completely different person than I was back then, I had developed a backbone and a 'take no shit' attitude. He may be able to bend me a bit, but he sure as hell wouldn't be able to break me again.

I wasn't stupid enough to poke a relaxed bear, but I could ruffle his feathers a bit until I could formulate a plan. The problem with creating an exit strategy on such short notice is that you can't foresee anything that would or could happen.

"Logan," I sneered through my clenched teeth. "Violating your parole so soon, are we?" I took a good long look at him. Back when we were married he was built like a brick shithouse, and could throw me over his shoulder like a battered and beaten ragdoll. But somehow he had gotten even bigger, if that was even possible. I could tell that he had made good use of the prison gym. His blond locks were overgrown in the way that I used to love, messy and disheveled. He could always just roll out of bed and run his fingers through his hair and look good enough to eat. He was clean-shaven, which just enhanced your focus on the cleft in his chin. I used to find it sexy and endearing, now it just left a bad taste in my mouth. I wanted to curl my lip at his entire appearance; what had I seen in him all those years ago? I wished I could blame it solely on being young and naïve, but I was also trying to find someone who would give me the love and nurturing I hadn't had growing up. Unfortunately, since I was still a stupid little girl, I had originally misconstrued Logan's domination as protectiveness. It took a long time and a lot of violence before I figured out that everything he did came from hate, not from love.

"Julia," he finally spoke, his tone laced with pure venom. I guess serving thirteen years of your sixty-year sentence made for some pretty intense sessions for your imagination on how he could retaliate. He took another step towards me and I tried to take another step back, but he had cornered me up against a wall. That was never a good thing. During the time I spent in therapy, they always told me never to let your attacker corner you with nowhere to go. Yeah, of course they could say that, they weren't up against the likes of Logan Wesson. His big hand came around me until he was grabbing my hair, tilting my face up so he could look down into my eyes. His fierce blue eyes were bloodshot and wild.

Was he on something?

"You've aged well, kitten," he said as he took in the length of my entire body. I always loathed that nickname he had for me.

"Yeah, well, you haven't." I spit back. Wasn't my finest moment, taunting him. But I needed to distract him. I knew that if I could make it around him by diving under one of his arms that was now caging me in, I could quickly grab my phone. Then there was the possibility of going past him on the left and darting out the front door.

"Don't even think about it, kitten. I see the wheels turning around in your head. You may have grown a mouth on you," he leaned in close, "but that just turns me the fuck on. The fact that you want to fight me, God, I could strip you down and fuck you right now. But you won't escape me. I won't allow it. The fact that you grew a backbone out of nowhere all those years ago and actually testified against me, well, you see that left a bad taste in my mouth. And now you're going to pay."

I wasn't terrified until that entire spiel left his mouth. A wave of unease washed over me as my heart rate picked up, my mouth went completely dry, and I couldn't help but to think that I wouldn't ever get to see Dean again. Or our baby. Over the past few days I had come to the conclusion that I wanted this child more than anything and I wanted it with Dean. I wanted to start a life together with him in Oregon. Because that's where I belonged, with him.

I had to try and fight; I couldn't just sit there and let Logan finally achieve the goal that I was sure he wished he had done all those years ago. I couldn't let him kill me.

Closing my eyes for just a brief moment and releasing a deep sigh, I wanted to make him think that I was succumbing to him, to do with as he wished, but then I immediately faked going left before rushing under his right arm, running as fast as I could into the kitchen. My eyes instantly honed in on my cellphone that was lying on the edge of my counter and I grabbed with one hand and frantically tried to punch in the code to unlock my phone with the other. I knew Logan was close but I wasn't expecting him to come up from behind me, his arm squeezing around my middle cutting off my air supply so I couldn't breathe.

"Little bitch," he growled as he gritted his teeth. Trying to use my feet, I kicked with all my might trying to break free so I could run off again. My phone was my lifeline as it remained tightly grasped within my clutch. I was able to type in my passcode and immediately my contacts appeared as if it was a sign. I knew that Dean couldn't rush here to save me, but he could call someone that could. It was hard to focus as my feet continued to thrash around and Logan's forearm was squeezing even tighter around my midsection. I had to get him to let me go.

I ceased all movement and went completely lax, thinking that he would release his grip around my stomach, which he did. He threw me to the ground and I scrambled with my phone, my finger hovering over Dean's name in my recently called list. The first blow landed directly square into my stomach with his foot. My breath whooshed out of me and I knew right then and there that I wouldn't be able to save our baby. I didn't even know if I had the option of saving myself.

My body's reaction was to curl in a ball as I released a loud, piercing scream. I screamed so loudly that my throat grew sore. He pushed me to my back with the same foot that had connected with my stomach just moments before and the last thing I remembered before waking up in the hospital was the knuckles on his right hand surging towards my face. The pain registered

behind my left eye after the velocity of impact just seconds before
everything faded to black.

My hand found my stomach again and I knew that the baby would be gone. There was no way that it could've survived after Logan. "The baby," I looked at Eden with tears swimming in my eyes silently conveying that I was thinking the worst and the pain that I was in was confirming it. I didn't think that the pain was solely due to Logan and his beating. She glanced down at my hand covering my abdomen, then sympathetically back up to me.

"Nurse, can she get an ultrasound to check on the baby, she's only a few weeks along." I wanted to pull Eden in for the biggest hug but I was afraid that it would just increase the pain radiating throughout my body.

"Can you please send Dean in here?" Eden just nodded in response and moved to the end of the bed, looking up at me. "Oh God," I whispered, "I must look awful." I wanted to cover my face with my hands. The thought of asking for a mirror crossed my mind, but I didn't want to face what would be staring back at me.

"Julia, you're beautiful. That man out there is crazy about you, he just wants to know that you're okay."

Okay. Well, wasn't that a loaded word. Within the next few minutes, I guess I should know the answer if I would ever be *okay* again.

Eden retreated out of my hospital room and I shifted in the bed, trying to make myself a little more comfortable. The nurse had left to retrieve the portable ultrasound machine. She stated that since I wasn't very far along it would be hard to hear the baby's heartbeat, so they needed to do the ultrasound internally. So I waited for Dean to make his appearance.

The first thing I noticed was his broad shoulder on his tall frame as he slowly eased his way into the room and when his eyes locked on mine, he stared for a beat. His nostrils flared and his jaw tightened, he squeezed his eyes shut and when he reopened them there was a delicate softness that hadn't been there before. He rushed over to my side and dropped to his knees, grasping one of my hands in both of his.

Bringing my hand towards his face, he dropped his lips to my skin, placing several closed-mouth kisses, sending burning desire through my flesh. He had yet to speak but his actions were loud and clear. He had dropped everything to be with me. To be by my side. That alone told me what I already kind of knew, but it had been made abundantly clear, solidifying my thoughts. He loved me.

Standing up, he bent over me, bracing his hand on the railing of my hospital bed and carefully dropped his forehead to mine. "Julia," he breathed. "It tore me up inside to think that I wouldn't ever get to relay to you my direct feelings. I love you, Julia Caldwell. I love you so much."

A sob threatened to break free from my scratchy throat. He loved me. Everything would be all right. Everything had to be all right.

The doctor entered the room and cleared his throat, "Ahem." Dean moved his head to reveal a short foreign man with dark hair and skin standing at the end of the bed glancing through my chart. "The nurse said that you are a few weeks pregnant but also experiencing some pain in your lower abdomen?"

I could see Dean's eyes snap to my face out of my peripheral, but I couldn't look at him. I nodded my head, "Yes, sir. I was kicked in my stomach before I blacked out so I don't know if the pain was from that or from..." I couldn't even finish the sentence, I refused to believe that our baby was gone.

"Well, the nurse did detect some mild bleeding when you were brought in, so I should be able to confirm whether or not you are miscarrying by a simple pelvic exam." He came around to sit on the end of the bed and lifted up the bottom of the blanket. His gaze found Dean's and he said, "Do you wish to stay?"

"You're not getting me to leave," Dean said, matter-of-factly. He grabbed ahold of my hand and wouldn't deter his eyes from mine during the entire exam. We just looked at one another while the uncomfortable prodding occurred.

"Just as I thought, you are in the process of miscarrying. The remaining tissue will be expelled completely through the bleeding, but we will want to monitor you in the hospital for a day or two more just to keep an eye on you. But then you'll be good to go. Oh, and now we'll be able to increase your pain medication if need be." He stood from the bed and snapped off his gloves with a 'thwak' before he tossed them into the trashcan on his way out. That jackass could definitely use a little brushing up on his Bedside 101 etiquette. He just told me that I was losing my baby in the same tone of voice he would use to order a fucking cheeseburger. With a little too much pep and completely no empathy.

I wouldn't ask for more pain medicine, I deserved all the pain I was in. Maybe the physical pain would help cover up all of the emotional. This time when a sob threatened to break free, I let it. Tears were heavily streaming down my cheeks as I looked up to Dean who stood there in shock, void of anything on his face except for the silent tears that fell.

"Dean?" My voice came out as a whimper and I didn't even recognize it as it sounded so dejected. After a moment he looked down at me and the hurt finally registered on his face. "I know I have no right to ask this, but will you...will you please come lay with me?"

I turned to my side and he carefully tucked himself behind me, making a conscious effort not to touch my IV line or to cause me any further discomfort.

For a few minutes there were no words spoken between us. He just held me while we cried together. For those single, solitary minutes, we could just *be*.

I was afraid to close my eyes because every time I did, Logan's image would appear. He took everything from me and I wanted him to pay.

When the police came back in the morning I would tell them everything I knew, but I hadn't made up my mind on whether or not I wanted to take matters into my own hands. Normally I was a ful' supporter of the police and allowed them to their jobs and serve justice, but look how well that worked out the first time.

"Every time I close my eyes, I see that bastard's menacing snarl." I was going to be afraid to look over my own damn shoulder. I refused to live my life in constant fear that some madman was lurking around in the shadows. And I refused that life for anyone I cared about as well. As hard as it would be, living life after having my baby ripped away from me, having to be without Dean, I had no other choice. I wouldn't put another innocent person in danger because of my past.

I had to let Dean go.

My body began to tremble as the sobs continued to flow. And Dean, God, I loved him, he just held onto me tighter. Admitting to myself that I was in love with Dean Parker made me cry that much more.

"Shh…" he said as he ran his fingers over my hair, it was soothing and I felt myself wanting to relax into his embrace but I didn't deserve to. "We're going to get through this together, sweetheart."

"I'm so sorry. I'm sorry for everything," I muttered through my tears. "It's pretty ironic, I suppose. At first I wanted nothing to do with the baby and once I began to love the idea, the decision was taken away from us. And all for what? So my jackass ex-husband could try and exact revenge on me? Well, he got it all right. He officially destroyed the rest of me."

Dean's hand still on my head, "You wanted the baby?"

My grief was consuming me and I barely managed to release the word in a whisper, "Yes."

Chapter 22

Dean

The mixture of hearing Julia cry and her admitting that she wanted the baby killed me inside. I had long since given up trying to keep my own tears at bay, allowing them to spill down my cheeks.

"I don't think I can manage to pick up the pieces again, Dean." Her voice came out so small and dejected, nothing like the Julia I knew and loved.

If only she needed me to chase away her demons, I would be the best damn bodyguard. But she was already withdrawing into herself, and fast. I was losing her and I didn't think that anything I said or did would change that.

"I'm a horrible person and when I finally had given my heart to having this baby, it was ripped away from me."

Ripped away from us.

I wanted nothing more than to find her ex-husband Logan and kill him with my bare hands for what he had done. I held her tightly in my arms, each of us mourning over what we had lost, until she asked me to leave.

Walking out of that hospital room, away from Julia, and down that long white corridor, took courage. Courage that I didn't know until then that I even possessed.

A piece of me died that day, I didn't know if she would ever contact me again, but in the end, no matter how much I argued against it, I had to respect her wishes to give her time.

When and if she called, I'd be there.

Chapter 23

Dean

Two long and lonely months had passed by and spring was upon us. I'd like to say that I kept in touch with Julia, but that would be a lie.

Ever since the day I walked out of the hospital with my tail between my legs, I vowed that the ball was in her court and would remain there. I wasn't going to keep trying to force something that may never be. No, if she wanted to talk to me, she would have to make the first move.

That wasn't to say that I never asked about her. I'd ask Eden from time to time for updates, to see if she'd heard from her and how she was doing, but I hadn't even bothered to ask the last few weeks.

Eden told me that Julia was pretty depressed over everything that had transpired but she wouldn't outright admit it. Two weeks ago I'd learned from a private investigator that I'd hired that Logan Wesson was found and would be charged accordingly. Since he had violated his parole within the first twenty-four hours of being released, he would never breathe the air as a free man ever again. Not that he should've been released in the first place.

My thought was that since Logan Wesson wasn't a threat to anyone any more, that Julia would try and contact me. She wasn't fooling anyone, she didn't want to put anyone else in danger over her past. I would have been doing the exact same thing, which was why I took matters into my own hands and hired a private investigator. It made me rest easier to know that he was keeping an eye on Julia for any signs of danger. The whole incident had proven to me that she did indeed care about me, although since I hadn't heard a peep from her in those two weeks, I was beginning to think differently.

My heart ached when I thought about her, which was quite often, but I wished it would stop. I wished I could turn my thoughts on and off like a switch, because quite frankly I was tired of the pain. My world had no color without her in it and I wished she would just reach out to me so we could talk things over.

For it being early April, the weather was unusually warm. Spring flowers were in full bloom and I already had to pull a massive amount of weeds that were growing in with my tulips around my mailbox.

Killing my lawn mower, I grabbed a rag out of my back pocket and wiped the sweat that had gathered along my forehead. I couldn't believe that I had to mow my lawn already, this wasn't looking promising as to how summer would go. But at least the yard work served as a pretty decent distraction.

My phone vibrated in my pocket and I almost dropped the damn thing on the pavement when I saw that it was a text...from Julia. My heart started racing, slamming against my ribs, threatening to beat right out of my chest. I couldn't get my fingers to work right, I was so nervous about what the message would say. I kept fumbling trying to open my text messaging app and had to actually pause to take a deep breath. I was such a pussy. Once I clicked on her name, the message appeared and my brows knitted together with vast confusion. What the hell did she mean?

Julia: Sledgehammer

My thumbs flew across my keyboard in record time and I was pressing send, asking to her to elaborate.

Dean: You want to take a sledgehammer...to my face?

In record time my phone was vibrating, alerting me of an incoming text from Julia. I smiled.

Julia: No, not today. That's what song reminds me of you. Sledgehammer.

I couldn't for the life of me think of how the song went, the beat, the melody, nothing. I was drawing a complete and total blank. So I went to the one person who would...Eden.

Running through our yards, I made my way in through the garage until I stopped in the kitchen. Even after running that short distance, I was still out of breath. I really needed to start working out more. I had to brace my hands on my knees just to catch my breath and suddenly this felt a little like déjà vu.

Eden took in my form with an amused expression on her face, her brows raised almost into her hairline as if she was saying, "Are you for real?"

"Uh, Dean, what's going on?"

"Eden! My musical genius best friend. How does Sledgehammer go?"

"Uh, how does a sledgehammer go, what? Are you all right?" she asked with a perplexed look. She probably thought I had turned to drugs or something equally stupid.

"No, the song, Sledgehammer. How does it go? I can't for the life of me think of it."

"Why do you need to know? And why couldn't you just look it up on your phone. You know, the electronic device that is currently attached to your hand?" Seriously? Couldn't this woman see that I was in a bit of a rush? She was throwing around questions that although made sense, didn't even initially cross my mind. I was losing patience.

"Eden..." I growled.

Shock registered on her face and her eyes grew wide, she picked up her phone and held up a hand in surrender. "Sheesh, hold on a minute, don't go all hulk on me." She tapped a few buttons and a few beats later the girl-band, Fifth Harmony, was filling the kitchen with their incredible song. Julia thought of me when she heard this song? Summing it up with a nicely colored bow, it basically said that her body told me that she wanted me but she just couldn't say the words. That her heart raced every time that she was near, but she kept things aloof, acting as if I didn't affect her in any way. This was Julia to a T.

I had to call her. I hightailed it out of there, throwing "Thanks," over my shoulder as I retreated back to my own side of the yard. I discarded my grass-stained shoes in my own garage, chastising myself for running into Eden's house with them on, and then maneuvered myself inside so I could sit at my kitchen table. I was sure that for this conversation I needed to be sitting down.

After only one ring, Julia immediately answered, the voice I missed and loved so much filling my ears, "Dean?"

I couldn't help the smile that spread across my face. She had reached out to me, all bets were off and I was going to lay the charm on thick. "I love the way you say my name," I teased.

"What took you so long to call?"

"Honestly? I had to run over and ask Eden to play the song for me. I'd heard it before but you put me on the spot and I couldn't think of any of the words. So that song really reminds you of me?"

She chuckled lightly, the sound hitting me directly below the belt. God, I missed her. "It does."

"So how are you?" I want to rapid fire off questions to her, asking her every single thing that came to mind, but I didn't want to overwhelm her.

"I'm better, I'm doing well. They found Logan two weeks ago and arrested him."

"That's great news, such a relief." I didn't want to explain to her that I already knew. She didn't need any leverage against me to use later on, so I just let it go.

"So," she started off kind of awkwardly, "are you seeing anyone?"

That question caught me completely off-guard. Did she actually think that I would go looking for someone else so quickly? There was no one else for me. "You know the answer to that, Julia."

I heard her release a deep sigh, was it a sigh of contentment? I wasn't sure. But then she said four little words that had my heart soaring in my chest, all the ache and pain forgotten. It made me appreciate the number four again, the curse had finally been broken. "I miss you, Dean."

Happiness was when the woman you loved, who you wanted to fully open her heart and mind to you, finally saw the light deep in her soul and professed that she missed you. Sure, it wasn't an undying plea of her love for me, but I'd take it. I would take it a thousand times over. Then maybe on one thousand and one, I'd make her at least tell me she loved me.

"You don't know how happy that makes me. Listen, I just got through mowing the grass and I need a shower. I'll call you later, yeah?" I could tell by her tone that she was a bit confused as to why I was trying to get off the phone so quickly. I had to set my plan in motion and I couldn't very well do that with her on the line.

This was the first time she had brought forth any kind of emotion. I was officially done waiting for her and what I was about to do could very well be the biggest move of my life. Only time would tell if I was doing the right thing.

Chapter 24

Julia

Logan was finally caught and arrested, so for the first time in almost two months, I could finally rest easy. Refusing to go back to my house where all the daunting memories would follow me around and haunt me, I rented a little apartment just down the block from Violet. My co-workers helped me in a tremendous way by packing up all my things and bringing them to my new place. My old house had sold just a few days ago so I didn't have to let the memory of being there hold me back.

Even though it had been two weeks since Logan Wesson was arrested, it took me a while to crawl out of my depression and I still wasn't quite one hundred percent, yet. But I needed to start living, really living. Not this floating along life with all these meaningless affairs that ultimately lead to a dead end. I used to think that if I never got involved with anyone else then I wouldn't have to actually *feel* anything towards them. Dean showed me that that wasn't a way to live. He showed me that I had lost myself along the way and he helped me find her again, the woman that I strived to be. He had been dealt a shitty hand in the Ex department same as me and he welcomed me with open arms. I had to learn on my own to do the same thing. Dean Parker ultimately made me want to be a better woman.

I had finally found someone who wanted me wholeheartedly, not just to love me but to take care of me. Being on my own for so long I had forgotten how good that felt, to be wanted. I tried everything in my power to push him away due to my hesitant reservations about what happened with my past. But living in the past wasn't how a person should live their life and from here on out I was only going forward.

Maybe Dean wouldn't want me anymore, but I had to try. I needed to lay everything out on the line and come out with every feeling and emotion I'd ever had around him even if it was foreign to me to do so.

Taking the first initial step had been nerve-wracking, but I made it through sending out the text message just fine. He responded so quickly there for a bit, but then after a few minutes with no response, I was beginning to get worried. Leave it to Dean to run next door and pester Eden about a song. I mean, she was a radio DJ, she had to know the popular songs. It made me smile just picturing it, I could see each step in vivid detail.

When his name popped up as an incoming call a tingle shot down my spine and I got all giddy. This feeling was much more pleasant when I wasn't trying to keep it bottled up; I let it all flow freely. Would he still irritate me? I sure hoped so. Bantering back and forth with him was some of the most fun I'd had in a very long time. We could have the most heated argument, screaming and yelling, but then that would make the making up part that much more sweet.

Admitting to him that I missed him took a lot of courage on my part. I didn't want to lay everything out on the line over the phone, but I needed to give him a sliver of hope. And while he said that he was overjoyed to hear me say that, it was almost as if he couldn't get off the phone with me fast enough. And the bullshit about him calling me back later…he had to be lying.

It had been a slow-ass day at work with time seeming to drag on little by little, and it didn't help that I kept staring at my phone, willing it to ring. That triggered something that my nanny always used to say, "A watched pot never boils." But she never had to say that in the context of waiting for the love of her life to call her back. I sent everyone else home and stayed late to make sure everything was in place and cleaned for the new manager to officially take over in the morning.

It was my last day at Violet Salon & Spa. I'd made this place my entire life for the past twelve years, but now I had changed and it just didn't feel right anymore. Maybe it was the location. Maybe it was because the people that I valued dearly weren't there to enjoy life with.

Did I know what my next step would be? Not exactly, but the thought of not having to be up early every morning to open up the Salon was exhilarating. I could sleep in as long as I wanted to, hang around in my pajamas all day if I wanted to; I had an infinite amount of options.

The lights were dim in the Salon and I was just finishing up sweeping up all the remaining hair that lingered on the floor, when I caught my reflection in the mirror. The purple rings under my eyes weren't as pronounced, and I guessed it was because I had a newfound energy to actually apply my makeup in the morning. I took in my new cut that Leila, one of my former employees, had done for me that afternoon. For as long as I could remember my hair had fallen down to the middle of my back, but I'd had a wild hair, a sudden impulse and wanted it cut. Now it fell to the tops of my shoulders in an angled bob with side-swept bangs. I let it dry naturally after my cut, so it curled around my face in soft waves. It was a drastic change, but one I felt I would become accustomed to in due time.

A new pop song filtered through the speakers we had installed into the ceiling and I found myself dancing a bit as I swept up the discarded hair.

Then suddenly the chime over the front door sounded, although I could have sworn that I had locked up after everyone left. The hair on the back of my neck stood up on alert and a sudden chill covered my exposed skin in goosebumps. I inched past my workstation where my purse was thrown on top of the counter and dug around until I found my phone.

Poised in my hand and ready to dial 9-1-1, I yelled out into the otherwise empty shop, "I'm sorry, but we're closed."

No answer.

I slowly crept around the partition that separated the front waiting area from the back of the Salon, with the numbers already dialed into my phone, just waiting on me to press that big green call button.

Once I took in the presence that was standing on the other side of the reception desk, my breath left my entire body in a rush. I squeezed my eyes shut really tightly, in case it was just a figment of my imagination. When I reopened my eyes, he was still there in all of his sexy glory.

Denim jeans that rested in the just the right position on his hips, and a black polo shirt that showcased his well-defined chest. He was clean-cut with his shirt tucked in and I felt the need to rush over and untuck it before tearing it completely off and dirtying him up a bit.

Dean.

He came for me.

I had just informed him yesterday that I missed him and today he totally showed up to surprise me. If that wasn't love, then I didn't want to be notified any different.

Tears of joy filled my eyes as my lips tipped up into the biggest smile I had ever shown to date.

I lingered at one end of the long oak reception desk, while he remained at the other. I noticed his eyes take their time roving up and down my body, making mine very aware at each part he landed on. He started with my feet, slowly traveling up my thighs, which tingled in his path. He seemed to pause for a moment on my abdomen, which made the butterflies flap around relentlessly. And I must admit, I was a little fuller in my midsection, due to my increased obsession with junk food and my decreased visits to Zumba, but he didn't seem to mind in the slightest. He then made his way up to my face, only pausing a short moment on my breasts. But when he finally stopped on my eyes, his own flared with an intense fire slowly burning at the sight of me.

Neither of us had spoken; we just let the silence hang between us until a small smirk played on the very edge of his lips. His signature cocky smirk. I knew what that signified and I knew what was coming out of his mouth even before he said it.

"You like me," he muttered, and crossed his arms in front of his chest as if he was finally triumphant, but there was also a hint of uncertainty as he held his breath.

I shook my head in response, making his smirk slide clean off of his face. But he hadn't even let me speak. "Wrong," I said, before quickly adding, "I love you." I ran over to the other end of the desk, where my love was waiting, catching him off-guard by jumping into his arms. He took a step back to brace himself before curling one hand around my back and fisting the other deep into my hair.

When my lips met his, I kissed him with all of the pent-up passion that I had held back on for so long. I expressed my deep, soulful love for him through that kiss. Mingling our tongues together, never coming up for air until we were each completely breathless.

He continued to hold me in his arms as I took my time kissing every inch of his exposed face with my fingers shoved in his overgrown hair.

"I'm so sorry, Dean. I've been the biggest hypocrite, because here I haven't been truthful. I said I never played games and it seemed as if I was stuck *trying* to lose the biggest game of my life, one that I should've been hell bent on winning from the beginning."

"I'm just glad you came to your senses. I didn't know how much longer I could've held off. I've missed this body of yours." His hand smoothed down my back until he was cupping my ass, eliciting a moan to escape from my throat.

I pulled on his unruly strands again, "Jesus, you need a haircut," I said in between kissing his lips again.

He smiled against my mouth, "Something tells me that I won't ever have to pay for a cut again. Say it again."

I bit his bottom lip, making him groan in appreciation. "What, that you need a haircut?" I joked, knowing exactly where he wanted this to go. "I love you. I love you. I love you, Dean Parker."

With me still in his arms, he walked around the partition to the solid wall on the other side, pressing my back up against it. I recalled a similar scene such as this that took place at Baylor and Eden's wedding, where we had our first kiss.

"You have a thing for walls, huh?"

He sat me down long enough to pull a condom out of his wallet, tore it open with his teeth as he pulled down his jeans and boxer briefs to his ankles before sliding it down his erect length.

Taking the material of my flowy, bohemian skirt in his fist he bunched it up around my waist, and shifted my panties over to the side. "No, baby, if you haven't already noticed, I have a thing for you." In the next instant he lifted me up against the wall again and immediately thrust himself into me until he was fully seated, my silkiness expanding to accommodate his size.

His eyes never left mine as he continuously thrust himself in and out of me, finally claiming me as his. "I love you, Julia."

I brought my hands up to cradle his cheeks, I kissed the center of his forehead, the tip of his nose, then his lips, "I love you so much, Dean."

His jerky movements picked up speed until I felt the all too familiar tingle as I was quickly nearing my orgasm. I closed my eyes, as my breathing came out in quicker pants, and leaned my head up against the wall, ready to succumb to the excitement. "Open your eyes," he bit through his clenched teeth. I snapped them open, obeying his command, and looked back into his eyes. His taut jaw and even faster thrusts told me that he too had almost reached his tipping point. "I want your eyes on me as we come."

One, two, three more thrusts and I moaned as my orgasm washed over me. Once he came down from his simultaneous high, he fell into me, bracing his arm on the wall while we each steadied our breathing.

"Wow," I said as I smiled when I could finally find my voice.

"I'll show you wow, I'm not done with you yet," he replied as he finally brought me to my feet, letting me regain my bearings before he let me go.

Rolling my eyes in his direction, "Promises, promises."

Later, after I had closed up the Salon for the night and made it back to my apartment, I found out just how much he wasn't done with me.

Epilogue

Dean

I could now count waking up next to Julia as my favorite place on earth. I really hadn't known what I was missing by not being able to sleep next to her, since last night was the first official night this had occurred between the two of us. And now that I had gotten a taste of it, there was no way I would ever go another night without her tucked into my side.

My right arm was thrown behind my head so I could get a better angle to look at her sleeping face. I'd been up for a while, and the tingling numbness in my left arm that she was laying on would say that it had been at least two hours. I didn't want to move an inch in fear that it would wake her up. She looked so peaceful with her light blonde lashes fanned out against her flawless, creamy skin. Her left arm was flung across my torso and curling into my side. Every now and again her fingers would twitch, tickling my ribs. It was so hard trying to keep still and when her fingers rubbed up against my exposed flesh it was pure torture.

She also pouted in her sleep. The first time I watched her lips plump up as they curved down into a frown, I wanted to immediately kiss them until she smiled again. Her nose twitched also, like a bunny; it was the cutest thing and made me fall in love with her all over again.

Her arm tightened around me as she started stirring awake. She tucked her head further into me, hiding her face completely from my view, but I could finally get my arm free and hopefully soon get some feeling back in it.

"Good morning, sleepyhead," I said as I leaned forward and planted a kiss on top of her exposed head.

She leaned up to the sound of my voice, not yet opening her eyes for the day, "Mmm, good morning," she said in her gruff morning voice, which I loved too. I was a damn sucker for this woman, there was no use even trying to deny it. She knew it, I knew it, and as soon as possible, all of Cottage Grove would know it.

Her eyes slowly fluttered open, trying to get used to the light that was peeking in through the curtains in her bedroom. The damn things were stylish, I supposed, but did nothing to keep the faintest glimmer of sunlight out, which was most likely the reason I was up so freaking early. Once her incandescent green eyes landed on mine, she smiled brightly before her expression turned to horror and she cupped her hand over her mouth.

Turning away from me, she allowed the blanket to fall to her waist, exposing her naked flesh. Damn, if I had remembered she was naked under the covers, I would've been staring at more than just her face for the past two hours. She tried lifting herself up with one arm to get out of bed, but I was having none of that. I curled my arm around the front of her stomach and hauled her ass back until she was tucked into my side once more. This time, her back to my front.

"Dean, let me go, I need to go brush my teeth. Morning breath is so fucking disgusting."

"Ah, I love a dirty mouth in the morning," I whispered into her ear. She wasn't going to leave this bed until I was ready for her to, and I knew she needed a little coercion to stay put. So I slowly slid the arm that was around her stomach down until my hand met the apex juncture of her thighs. Having her totally at my mercy wouldn't hurt for my next topic of conversation, either. Her breath hitched as I brought my fingers through her curls and she even opened her legs a bit for easier access on my end. Most likely it wasn't to help me out, but rather for her own greedy needs.

I found her opening, which was already ready with hot, slick desire, and she moaned then whimpered when I pressed one digit, then two deep into her pussy.

"I'm keeping you in bed forever. Although, I'd much rather us be in my bed back in Cottage Grove." I curved my fingers and felt around until I found the one spot that made her tense up. Massaging it a bit, she quickly relaxed and as I opened my mouth to say something else, she surprisingly interrupted me.

"Ok…"

I stilled my fingers inside of her, "Wait, what?"

She tried wiggling around, grinding her ass into my fully erect cock, trying to get me to move my fingers again. "O-k. I'm on board, let's go. But you have to finish what you started first."

I removed my fingers from her pussy completely because I had to make sure she was fully coherent with what she just agreed to. She pouted and released an annoyed whimper, as I moved to sit up and roll her completely onto her back. "Just like that?"

Her eyes narrowed on me before she replied, "What do you mean, just like that? We've been going back and forth with this same song and dance since mid-December."

"Actually it was September when I first saw you, at your Salon before Eden moved to Oregon. My heart whispered, *she's the one*."

She brought her hand up and smacked my upper arm, harder than I'd like to admit. Which wasn't the exact reaction I was looking for. "You are so full of shit. Why I love you, I'll never know," she pretended to be mad, crossing her arms over her chest, which just lifted her breasts, exposing those pink-dusted nipples of hers.

I licked my lips and brought my hand to my chest, acting as if she wounded me. "Why do you?" I shrugged my shoulders, then to just clarify, "love me?"

"Because you forced me to. Never let up. Made me see the error of my ways." She was completely blowing smoke up my ass, but I would let it slide for now.

"I quit my job, so I'm free to do anything I wish."

"Quit your job, rather presumptuous aren't we?" I relished the fact that I could throw her statement back in her direction.

She shrugged a shoulder, acting extremely nonchalant about the entire conversation, but I knew she was just as nervous as I was, "I guess I can suffer the permanent frizz ball my head will become because of the rain and gloom. Maybe my presence will add some flair to the otherwise desolate town." She looked down, before looking straight back into my eyes. And this time I could see completely into her soul, nothing standing in her way. "And besides, I'm ready to start my life with you."

That was it, she said the words, now it was time to put things into motion. I jerked up off of the bed, still completely naked, and intertwined our fingers together, trying to pry her from the mattress.

"What are you doing?" She muttered, surprised by my actions.

"Come on. We've got work to do. We need to pack your bags, it's time for us to go home." My smile shown so brightly, I couldn't even contain how happy I was that I finally got the girl.

I had Julia Caldwell right where I wanted her and we had the rest of our lives to express all of the ways we loved each other. Our official life together could finally begin...once we landed back on Cottage Grove soil. I for one, couldn't wait.

Julia

It was now Saturday night and we, along with Baylor and Eden, decided to head over to Tillie's for a few drinks. I seemed to be settling in fine over the past several days; the hardest part was just trying to get used to living with a man again. Luckily for me, Dean made it fairly easy.

I never thought I would ever let that happen again after what I went through with Logan and Paul. But Dean opened my eyes to how good it could be and so far, it was actually going really great. Now, mind you it'd only been a handful of days, but I was hopeful for what was to come.

We kind of had a routine going the past few days. I would cook dinner and have it ready by the time he came home from work, and since I cooked, he would clean up the dishes. Each time he would be elbows deep in soap suds, I would remember back to that time in Eden and Baylor's kitchen. A knowing smile would form on my lips and Dean would just wink, telling me that his thoughts didn't stray far from my own.

I liked that he wasn't a slob, actually relished in the fact that I wasn't always trailing after him picking up empty beer bottles or discarded socks, so keeping the house picked up and clean wasn't a real chore. Then normally after dinner we would try to maul one another and see who could get out of their clothes the quickest. The funny thing was, I would always win. He'd come in with his discarded suit jacket and already have his cufflinks off, but he still had the matter of his buttoned-up dress shirt, under shirt, plus his slacks. Me, I would find different ways to cheat. I never claimed to play fair. Since I had been home most, if not all day, I would flaunt around in a pair of leggings, and a T-shirt without a bra, so it was pretty easy for me to shimmy out of my clothing. Then there was the day where I met him at the door with nothing but my bathrobe on...yeah, dinner had to be reheated that night.

Wash, rinse, repeat as the days went on. But it was never monotonous as one would think doing a lot of the same things day in and day out. I actually found that I enjoyed seeing him off to work and being there when he got home. Who knew that I would actually look forward to and didn't flinch at the term, housewife?

No, we didn't run off to get married, nor had we even discussed it. But if and when the time came, I wouldn't be scared of marrying a third time anymore because Dean was it for me.

How did that old saying go? "Third time's the charm?" That definitely held value between the two of us.

Dean's hand shifted underneath my dress and covered my bare knee, bringing me out of my reminiscing of this past week. I placed my hand over his before directing my attention to my right and on him.

"Whatcha thinking about, sweetheart?" His tone was gentle and it amazed me how his voice could make my stomach flip. I knew I could listen to the sexy timber of his voice for hours.

I put my elbow on the table in front of us and cradled my chin in my free hand and gave him a slight smirk. "Oh, I was just thinking about when we came here after I first got into town back before their wedding," I indicated over to Baylor and Eden with my eyes. "And how we've flipped a complete one-eighty since then."

"I for one am glad of the direction you two took. This outcome is way more enjoyable," Eden chimed in with a smirk from my left.

"Oh come on, we weren't *that* bad towards one another," Dean interrupted, instantly on the defensive.

Eden quirked a brow while Baylor belted out a laugh. "Yeah, I'm going to call you on your bullshit right there." He glanced over to me, "You guys were awful, so much tension and animosity. Who knew that this," he indicated with his hand to Dean and myself, "would be the outcome of a fling."

216

Eden raised her hand before bringing it behind my back, "I don't care what it took to get to this point. The past is in the past, I'm just glad that my best friend is now here with me in Cottage Grove. And what's better, she lives right next door."

Her smile quickly faded and I knew she was about to address the elephant in the room. The fact that I never really brought up any plans to try and have another child wasn't at all lost on her. I steeled myself for the conversation as it could go either way. "Have you two talked about the possibility of trying to have a baby?"

Now that I had gone through part of the mindset of having a child, before the decision was abruptly taken away from me, I absolutely had no qualms about trying again.

I looked over at Dean and his loving smile as he squeezed my knee, "We have discussed the topic again. And we feel that if it's meant to be, then it will be. I'm not against having a baby, in fact I would be thrilled." This was one of the first things that Dean and I discussed in depth when we returned to Cottage Grove. I knew I was getting older and would be turning thirty-six soon, so there would be risks to take and if it were to happen that I would stay at home during the pregnancy.

"What are we thrilled about?" Bentley appeared on the other side of Dean, his appearance a disheveled mess. His hair was laying in various wayward directions and part of his polo shirt was untucked from his jeans. He looked as if he came straight from a bathroom hookup.

"Jesus, Bentley, do you ever keep it in your pants?" Baylor admonished.

Bentley glanced down at himself and then shrugged a shoulder, "Actually, I have." He looked around the table at our surprised expressions regarding his admission. "Yeah, I can't believe it either," he muttered rolling his eyes. What in the world was going on with him? It was obvious with the dark circles under his eyes and the few days worth of stubble that he hadn't been sleeping well.

Wait…

"Well, color me surprised, Bentley Jenkins is wrecked over a woman. Never thought I'd see the day," Dean chuckled, as he lifted his glass of bourbon towards his mouth only to have it removed from his hand by Bentley.

"What the…" Dean growled as he jerked his head towards the drink snatcher.

Oh no, this wasn't good. Dean wasn't Bentley's biggest fan on a good day, but this would no doubt end messily.

He took a small drink, "I'm not wrecked over a fucking woman," his defenses were on high alert and he responded a little too quickly. Hmm…

He signaled for the waiter that was in our section, thankfully it wasn't Maisie, and raised Dean's mostly empty glass in the air towards him. "Can we get two more of these?" he asked before he quickly tossed the rest in the back of his throat.

"Yeah, for some reason I don't believe you," Baylor goaded.

Bentley pulled out one of the remaining two chairs and flopped himself down into it. "Believe what you want, brother of mine," he responded gruffly.

There was an internal war raging in Bentley's head that he didn't want anyone to notice. Everyone around me carried on with their conversations, ignoring the new person at our table, which I think was the norm for Bentley. He constantly lived in Baylor's shadow, getting cast aside. But not by me, I just sat back and watched him.

A few moments later, his head looked up as he gazed past me, his eyes widened with shock before his body flinched. He silently cursed, "Fuck," under his breath. If you hadn't been watching him directly, then you would've missed the entire thing.

I turned around to see exactly what his eyes were transfixed on and it didn't surprise me in the least to learn that it was Miri, who appeared to be here with another man. Her eyes were equally as wide and equally as transfixed on him. Now, I hadn't seen Bentley since the night of the wedding, and I had no idea what went on, if anything at all. But when I turned back around and focused my attention on Bentley, there was no doubt in my mind that he was hurting.

His deep brown eyes flashed to mine and I could see the underlying heartache lingering in their depths. I tried to give him a small smile, but he quickly shook his head. He knew that I was aware that there was something was going on, but he wanted to leave it at that.

My heart ached for what Bentley must be going through. Hopefully in the end, everything would work out the way it was supposed to.

Eden's excitement brought my attention back to the table, "You know what I just realized, Jules?" I honestly hadn't a clue, so I just shook my head. "You and I finally got our happy ever after."

Bentley hastily chimed in with his two cents worth, "Happy ever afters are for fucking losers." He quickly downed his glass of bourbon and stormed off from the table.

I could see Dean's hands clench on the table out of the corner of my eye and I just knew he was itching to go after him. I covered his hand with mine and just shook my head, "Let him go, he's in obvious pain and needs to work things out himself."

Dean's expression turned perplexed, "What are you talking about?"

I looked over to Eden whose eyes told me she understood what was going on, and I turned back to Dean, "I'll fill you in later, let's just have fun between the four of us."

We sat back and finished up the rest of our drinks. If you had told me months ago that I would end up falling head over heels madly in love with a divorce lawyer, I would've laughed in your face and told you to take a hike. But love had a funny way of finding you even when you weren't looking, or in my case, didn't even want it. I supposed Eden was right, we did find our happy ever after. It took me a long time to realize that I could be happy again, and I was just glad that I finally listened to what my heart had wanted all along.

I glanced over at Dean to see him already watching me intently, a smile on his face so bright that it made the corners of his eyes crinkle. The insurmountable love that was directed towards me was unmistakable and I found myself leaning in his direction, bringing my lips to his. He met me halfway and we shared a kiss that I would never grow tired of. It was soft and gentle and wasn't rushed. But in that kiss, it told me everything that I already knew, and once he pulled away and my eyes fluttered open, he let me know once again, "I love you Julia. I'm so happy that I made you see that all of this," he swept his hand down the length on his body, "was worth more than just a fling."

He sure knew how to lay it on thick, but I loved him for it. I rolled my eyes, and muttered "You have one hell of an ego there, Mr. Parker. Pretty sure of yourself, huh?"

But he knew he was right, he did show me that what we had together was definitely worth more than a fling.

About The Author

Amber is a stay at home mom currently residing in Southern Indiana with her husband and two beautiful daughters. If she's not shopping, going to concerts or on road trips, or having her nose stuck in a book, you'll often find her at the ball field watching one of the numerous sports that her girls are involved in.

Contact Amber

Facebook: www.facebook.com/ambernationauthor

Email: ambernationauthor@gmail.com

Twitter: @nation_amber

Website: www.ambernationauthor.com

Acknowledgements

My family: Jarrod, Alexis, and Olivia- I say this each and every time but it still holds true. Thank you so very much for believing in me and continuing to stand behind my decision to write and following my own dreams. I love you three to the moon and back!

Savannah Stewart: I don't know what I would do without you in my life. I am so thankful that we've crossed paths due to the Indie community. Thank you for being such a great friend, one that I truly feel that I can rely on. Love ya, lady!

Mayas Sanders: I feel I can always come to you and you'll give it to my straight up. Thank you so much for always being first and foremost taking a chance on my writing and my books. I appreciate you more than you may ever know and am so thankful to have you in my corner.

Ashley Volk: Thank you so much for your continued encouragement and support. I can always count on you to give me an honest and straight forward opinion before I release to the rest of the world.

Najla Qambar: It all started with a premade cover and has grown into an amazing series of beauty. I absolutely love all the work you do and can't wait to see what the future holds for us.

Jen Akers: You, my friend, are an editing master! I appreciate all of your hard work in making my books the best they can be. And I now know that it is all right, not alright. LMAO!

Enticing Journey Book Promotions: Thank you so much for your continued hard work. I cannot express just how much I appreciate all that you do.

READERS, AUTHORS, and BLOGGERS: **THANK YOU SO MUCH** for taking the time to read and review *More Than A Fling* and not only for taking a chance on *Dean* and Julia, but for any of my books that you've chosen to read. Without the readers, we are nothing. So I greatly appreciate all of your continued encouragement and support. **MUCH LOVE TO EACH AND EVERY ONE OF YOU!**